THE DAGGER'S CURSE

D1102061

The Fergus and Flora Mysteries

THE DAGGER'S CURSE

Wendy H Jones

Books to Treasure

Books to Treasure
5 Woodview Terrace,
Nailsea, Bristol, BS48 1AT
UK

www.bookstotreasure.co.uk
www.facebook.com/BooksToTreasure

First edition 2016

Text © Wendy H Jones
Design and layout © Books to Treasure
Cover illustration © Ken Dawson

Printed in the UK by Latimer Trend
9 8 7 6 5 4 3 2 1

ISBN 978-1-909423-64-0

The Dagger's Curse

Ammon slipped away from the smell of rotting flesh. So many decomposing bodies. They had to be buried in history's first mass grave. He moved slowly at first; then, once on the edge of the battlefield, he ran. Fled into the night, hidden by darkness so deep it could smother a man. The sound of the leather of his stout sandals slapping against the ground reverberated through the night. Dust leapt from the dry earth and choked him. He stopped. Coughed. Breathed in the scent of human excrement. There were middens near, signifying habitations. He dared not approach. This meant certain death. They would hand him over to the Pharaoh. Mentuhotep had no time for men who dodged their duty. That duty was to die for the king. Ammon did not want to die. The loud rasping of his breath called out like a griffin screeching in the night. Still he did not stop. He dared not.

He reached his house, fell through the doorway and collapsed. He heard screaming. His brain could not take in who it was or what it was for. Hands pulled at him and dragged him up against the wall. His wife, Nefret. At sixteen years of age, society considered him an adult. Old enough to fight. Old enough to marry. Yet young enough to feel terror. He felt his wife stroke the skin of his cheek, rough and chapped from exposure to the scorching sun and the desert wind. Soothe him, despite the dirt and the blood. The blood of his friends who had died or been left behind on the battlefield. He could hear the shrieking and groaning still, an echo of the battlefield bouncing around in his brain, threatening to explode. It would never go away. He could feel the rough brick wall of the main room through his tunic. It supported him in his exhaustion. His wife thrust a stone jug of beer into his hand. He grabbed it, eager to slake his thirst. Liquid ran down his chin and splashed the front of his tunic as he gulped. He turned to the food she offered and stuffed it down, almost choking in his haste.

His hunger sated, he staggered into his workroom. Stone jars held the tools of his trade, poisons such as arsenic, opium, strychnine and hemlock. Before his forced march to war, he had been a master at distilling the rare poisons. This was of no interest to Pharaoh, who required strong men for his armies. Now it would come in useful. A measured amount from each jar was poured into a clay bowl. Pulling out a small dagger, he studied it. Intricate, it was a thing of great beauty. A beauty which contained a murderous underbelly. He dipped the blade in the poison three times. With each descent he chanted the curse.

> "Sakhmet conjure up your daimons,
> as many as a plague of locusts,
> khayty, the daimons of darkness,
> bring forth their might,
> in power bring pestilence and affliction,
> may death be upon those who touch this blade,
> in protection throughout time,
> those who own it will be saved."

Dip. Pause. Dip. Pause. Dip. Too important to rush, the most powerful curse in the land was sealed. The passage of centuries could not break it. A curse of protection: its owner would be untouched. Any person, from peasant to Pharaoh, who tried to break the bond between owner and dagger, would die. This would not be a pleasant death, but one too horrible for human imagination. No one would dare unleash the curse.

Chapter 1

Flora MacDonald pressed her face and hands against the glass of the shiny new display case. With her fluorescent orange T-shirt she looked like a tabby cat sliding down a window. She was sweating like a lamb in a lion's cage, leaving smears all over the clean glass. Her eyes were fixed on the contents of the case.

Stace McIntyre picked at the edge of her shellacked nails as she gazed at the ceiling. "Bor-r-ring. Only sunny day we've had this year and we're stuck in a crummy old museum."

Flora swivelled round and elbowed through the crowd of school kids towards the offender. "Enough with the talking, loudmouth. You might have the IQ of a slug, but some of us are listening."

"Yeah. Shut it," Tegan Gloag joined in. "Some of us want to learn. Do you want me to tell you what that means?" Her blonde ponytail swung in time to her words.

The others shuffled round, their eyes brimming with expectation. A bunch of fourteen and fifteen year olds with teen concerns, they were anticipating a fight.

Someone whispered: "Might liven things up!"

Flora tightened her fists in readiness in case it kicked off. Although not one to start a fight herself, she didn't mind taking precautions.

The vaulted ceilings of the vast, almost empty hall of the museum picked up their voices and bounced the sounds off the thick stone walls in booming echoes. The sun had kept most people away despite the dagger's popularity.

Mrs Brannigan, their history teacher, whipped round and glared at them. "Girls! One more word out of you and the whole class gets detention."

Muttering broke out, leading to a sharp "*Quiet.*"

Flora turned back to the guide who was telling them about the dagger. This one display was the only reason they were here at all. A temporary exhibit, it was on loan from the Museum of Egyptian Antiquities in Cairo. Dundee was one of the few places in Scotland where it would be shown. Flora and her bestie, Fergus, hung on to every word. Not that Fergus needed to. *He* could have given the spiel in its entirety, with embellishments.

"Most folks think this dagger is unremarkable," the guide was saying. "They're right. In many ways it would be difficult to distinguish this from any other four-thousand-year-old Egyptian dagger."

Flora sidled up to Fergus, avoiding the beady eye of their teacher.

"He's right. It just looks like a lump of old metal. It could do with a bit of a clean. The gold handle's a bit of all right, though."

"It's as clean as it's gonna get," replied Fergus. "It's been buried in a tomb for a few thousand years. No one was going around with a bottle of household cleaner."

"You might want to gather in closer for this next bit," said the guide.

He gave time for the shuffling and jostling to end.

"What makes this different—" he paused and pointed to some tiny engravings on the blade "—are those hieroglyphics."

A slew of eye-rolling and mutters followed this amazing revelation. The word on the street said that this old lump of metal was amazing. That it was like no other dagger in the history of the universe. Daggers were all fine and dandy: you could kill people with daggers. Hieroglyphics were another thing altogether. They were like school.

Flora couldn't believe that they didn't get it. The hieroglyphics were what this outing was all about. She and Fergus held their breath.

The guide, knowing he was about to make their day, grinned and continued, "These hieroglyphics tell of the curse that was laid on this blade. A curse which continues to the present time."

Heads snapped up and the pupils leaned in closer.

"This is beginning to get exciting."

"No' half bad for a school trip."

"What's this curse then?" Even Stace had moved her gaze from the ceiling. "We're dying of boredom waiting for you to give us the skinny."

"That is quite enough of your cheek, Miss McIntyre." Despite the reprimand, Brannigan was smiling.

Flora leaned closer to Fergus and said, "Teacher's pet gets away with it again. Must be good having Teach as your aunty."

"There will be severe consequences for anyone who comes into contact with it," said the guide.

"What sort of consequences? Could we use it on Fergus, Geek of the year?" Stace cast a challenging look in his direction.

That was the wrong thing to say. Flora's temper matched her hair: short and spiky. She waded in to protect her friend.

"Shut it or I'll rearrange your face. Just because he doesn't want to go out with a skank like you."

Flora's voice rose with the same speed and ferocity as her temper. Mrs Brannigan snapped around.

"Flora MacDonald, my office when we get back to school."

Flora thought about how good it would be to land one right on Brannigan's fat little nose. Her only consolation: school finished today. Seven weeks free of hockey, netball and Brannigan.

The guide continued. "To answer your question about

consequences, young lady. Dire consequences indeed. Everyone who handled this blade lost their life, their kingdom or their authority. This is one of the most powerful curses that has ever been known."

Flora prayed that Stace would somehow touch it and do the world a favour.

Chapter 2

This dagger was the ultimate prize. The minute they heard it was coming to Dundee, the plan started to germinate. They scoped out the Victorian gothic building from every conceivable angle. Standing proudly in the middle of Dundee, the museum was floodlit 24/7 and protected by a number of alarms. This heist would not be easy but neither was it impossible.

Three hundred and fifty notes changed hands and a deal was made. A power cut was arranged, 0230 to 0240.

At the appointed time a figure nipped behind the statue of Queen Vic. A couple of twists and the door opened. A switch was thrown, shutting off the alarm to the relevant display cabinet. Two steps, another couple of twists and the dagger was liberated and placed carefully in an attaché case.

The route was reversed and as the figure disappeared from view, the power cut ended. The perfect crime had just taken place. Dundee slept, little knowing the evil that had been unleashed.

The next morning the city awoke to the ringing of phones and the shrill ping of text messages. The news was out. The dagger stolen. The curse unleashed. What would become of the city and its inhabitants? No one, old or young, was safe. A reign of terror had begun.

Chapter 3

Fergus could tell something was up. His parents, who included him in everything, were whispering in corridors. Fergus tried every which way to find out what was going on. At five foot ten and a half, and wearing nothing but shorts and his shaggy hair, it was difficult for him to blend into the shadows. Keen though his hearing was, the listening at door thing wasn't working either. Not even when he used the old glass trick.

"Not now, Fergus." His dad, Duncan, wiped sweaty hands on his trousers. The sweat mingled with the dirt to form muddy slashes. He glanced at his hands and wiped them again. His dad was used to mucky palms. A world-famous archaeologist, he was never happier than when on his knees in dirt-filled excavation sites. Worry was not the usual expression plastered across his face.

"I can help."

"Fergus, I haven't got time for this. Go to your room."

"But …"

"Fergus. Enough."

Fergus lived in the one and only turret room in the house. All of his many siblings had vied for it, but despite being the youngest, he had won the fight by dint of the fact that his father was on his side. It was the biggest room and Fergus was as good as his father at collecting artefacts. It was his own private enclave of privacy and peace. Not a parent or a brother to be seen. But there was little peace this night. He trudged up the winding stairs to his room, his feet heavy with the weight of his parents' problems. Sometimes it sucked, being a teenager. He switched on his iPhone docking speaker and Leturgica blared out. The music stilled his whirling thoughts and suckiness flew out of the open window.

Flora threw herself on her bed. "Why can't I have a normal mum like everyone else? It's so not fair."

Her spaniel, Charlie, jumped up beside her and cuddled in close. Flora stroked the dog's soft ears. Charlie usually calmed her right down, but he was failing in his duties today. She picked up a stuffed bunny her sister had left behind and flung it at the wall. It smacked into her overflowing bookcase and a couple of books landed with a crash on the floor.

"What did I do to deserve her?" she whispered into the dog's ear. The spaniel responded by licking her nose.

The sound of a FaceTime call took her mind off the general unfairness of life.

"Fergus, wassup. My mum's grounded me for a hundred years."

"What you done now?"

"Nothing. She's so mean."

"You still must have done something. Even your mum's not that bad."

"She said I didn't clean my room."

"Your room always looks like a herd of elephants rampaged through it. Followed by a herd of wildebeest just to make sure. I'd say she was right."

The flatness of Fergus voice penetrated Flora's sulk and she looked at him intently. "What's up with you?"

"My parents are hiding something."

"*Your* parents. No way! They're the most perfect parents in the whole wide world."

"Yes way. They've got faces like sucked lemons. I'm worried, Flora."

"Do you want me to come over?"

"You're groun—"

Fergus realised he was talking to himself. Flora hadn't bothered waiting for his reminder. She'd hit end call and no doubt was halfway through the door already.

The sound of a bicycle clattering to the ground some time later startled Fergus from his reverie. No, make that two bikes. Flora had her sister with her. The racing slap of footsteps was heard on the winding stairs, then the pair barged into his room.

"Hi, Arabella."

"It's Bella. You know that, Fergus." Grinning, she loped over to Fergus's computer and picked up the mouse. "Can I go on the 'puter?"

Bella had blonde hair, a sunny nature, and Down's syndrome. Despite her eleven years, she had a reading age of six and yet an ability with computers that was uncanny.

"Fill your boots."

Bella giggled. "I'm wearing shoes, Fergus." The girl signed in and was soon apparently oblivious to the pair of them.

"Mum's at the mean drunk stage. I couldn't leave Bella with her."

Their father was away on one of his numerous business trips, leaving Flora on 'Bella duty'.

"So what's going on?" she asked.

"No idea. They're not saying."

"Don't tell me you haven't listened in. Are you losing your touch?"

"Tried. They sent me packing. Did half hear something about friends making sly digs. People saying Dad's got keys to the museum."

"Nah. That wouldn't faze them. Specially since your dad didn't do anything. Murdoch isn't doing drugs again, is he?"

Fergus's big brother's teen years had not gone smoothly. He was the blackest of black sheep. The paths of his past were littered with drugs, theft and police cells.

"Nah. He's joined the church crowd. He's a changed man."

"I didn't even see your parents when I came in. Your mum's usually there offering me some veggie treat."

"Fergus, why are you sad?" came from the direction of the computer. Bella wasn't quite so oblivious as she had seemed.

"I'm fine, Bella. Specially since seein' you."

Bella flashed her beaming smile and turned back to defending the galaxy.

Over the noise of shooting and explosions they thought they heard the screech of cars.

"Was that noise for real, or on Bella's game?" asked Flora.

Fergus dashed over and peered out.

"Police cars."

The chiming doorbell was followed by the clatter of urgent footsteps.

"Flora, come on." Fergus dashed through the door.

"Bella, stay there."

Flora thundered down the winding stairs to the vast hallway below. Arriving at the ground floor, she was greeted by the sight of Duncan, in handcuffs and flanked by a pair of no-nonsense bobbies.

"Call our lawyer. She'll get it sorted out. I'll be home soon."

Fergus's mum, tears streaming down her face, could only manage a nod.

Flora grabbed Fergus's hand and he grasped it as though it could save the world.

Chapter 4

Flora dragged herself out of bed at sparrow's fart the next morning. Her mum was sleeping off the night before. Her father had come home at some ungodly hour, so she was safe to leave Bella. She gave her sister some cereal and sat her in front of the telly. That would keep her occupied for hours. She threw on the brightest clothes she could find in an effort to outdo the weather. She grabbed her favourite yellow shorts and, because she'd lost some weight and they were a bit too big, she riffled through her drawer, and pulled out a multi-coloured leather belt. *Perfect.*

Downhill all the way, it only took her twenty minutes to reach Fergus's grand home. She threw some chuckie stones at his window. Quite a feat given its distance from the ground. A few rattles told her they'd hit their target. The window opened and a bare-chested Fergus stuck his head out.

"Let me in."

A couple of minutes later she was in the kitchen. Fergus poured muesli into two bowls, and some ice-cold orange juice into glasses.

"Have you not got any *decent* cereal?"

"What do you think?" He handed her a spoon and a large tub of yogurt.

"You could at least keep some in for friends." She resigned herself to her fate and shovelled a heaped spoonful of breakfast into her mouth. *Maybe if I eat it quick it will taste like cocoa pops.* She gulped down the orange juice.

"That juice is the biz. It's hot as Hades out there."

"Never mind what grub we have in the house. What are we going to do about my dad?"

"What's he been arrested for?"

"Stealing the dagger."

"What? You're kidding, aren't you?"

"Nope. They said it had to be an inside job. Dad has a key to the museum, as he does a lot of work with them."

"Didn't he discover the dagger in the first place?"

"Yeah. Him and a bunch of Egyptians. That's why it came to Dundee."

"If it was him, wouldn't he have stolen it earlier? Before it got to Dundee, I mean."

"The police said it was easier for him to nick it here. Well, so the lawyer says."

"Jeez." She paused and then added, "Do you think your dad might have done it?"

Fergus leapt from the chair and she sat bolt upright ready to flee. She'd never seen him this mad.

"Shut up! Just *shut up*! No *way* he would do that."

"I know, all right. Sorry."

Fergus slumped back on the rickety kitchen chair, which creaked as his bottom thumped down. When it came to furniture, his parents were the make-do-and-mend type.

"I'll tell you what we're goin' to do. Solve the crime, of course," said Flora.

"Are you mad? We're not exactly the Famous Five." Fergus got up and stuffed a couple of slices of organic pumpkin seed bread in the toaster.

"No, we're the dynamic duo."

"That's Batman and Robin."

"Okay. How about Fergus and Flora, the Detective Duo. We could be like Sherlock Holmes and Watson."

"This is serious, Flora. We can't go off half assed. We'll make things worse."

"How could it be worse? Your dad's in jail."

"*We* could get arrested."

Conversation halted while they smeared honey on the toast. Fergus scraped a drop off the wooden table with his knife.

Once they'd finished munching, Flora continued, "I wish we *would* get arrested. I'd get away from my crazy mother. Anyway my great blah blah grannie, the original Flora MacDonald, never worried about that. She was thrown in the Tower of London for rescuing Bonnie Prince Charlie. The most we'll get is a telling off from the local coppers."

"So we've got a name. What do we do now, smart ass?"

"How come *I've* got to do all the work?"

"We work, Detective Flora. *We* work. That's us, not just me, in case you haven't realised it. Besides, it's your idea!"

Despite the teasing tone, Fergus felt a tiny ray of hope struggle to emerge. Maybe there *was* something they could do.

Chapter 5

The Detective Duo needed more information so they went to find Fergus's mother in her studio. She was daubing scarlet and black paint on a huge canvas. The ferocity of her strokes splashed the paint hither and thither. Specks of it gave certain jauntiness to her otherwise grey hair. Her dachshund, Hatshepsut, was curled up in a corner. Multi-coloured paint adorned her fur like a flamboyant Indian headdress.

"Mum."

The artist swung round and a stray blob of red landed on Flora's hoodie.

Wiping it off, Flora said, "Hi, Rad."

Rad—alias Ariadne—smiled. "Flora. Is Fergus looking after you?" Her usually friendly voice was weak. She rubbed at eyes already red, streaking the lids with black. By the looks of the palette, she was using any colour she could get her hands on.

"Yeah. I'm good—"

Fergus butted in on the pleasantries. "Why are you painting? Shouldn't you be down the station getting Dad out?"

His mum strode in his direction waving her brush around. Cue more flying paint.

"Of course I should. You'd think I'd be hard at it. But no, the police won't release him, so I'm stuck here painting and waiting for his lawyer to sort it out."

"What's going on with Dad, anyway? We need more info."

"I've already told you. I don't need to repeat myself."

"That's too weird. Dad wouldn't steal any artefact, never mind one as important as this. What makes them think he did?"

"I don't know, Fergus. The police aren't telling me anything." She turned back to the canvas and the wild strokes resumed.

Flora opened her mouth but Fergus shot her a "no more" look and indicated the door with his eyes. Flora took the hint.

The minute they entered Fergus's room, Flora stripped off her hoodie and threw it on the floor. It lay in a defiant pose in the otherwise fairly neat room. Flora's mother wasn't the only one cracking the "tidy your room" whip.

Pulling at her bright orange Leturgica T-shirt, Flora said, "Have you got the heating on?" The T-shirt was a souvenir from the concert they'd both gone to earlier in the year. The band had epic status in both their lives, and the concert had been Fergus's birthday present.

"Nope."

"Think I'll go sit in the oven. Has to be an improvement on this."

"It's not that bad." Fergus's sweat-stained shirt gave the lie to his words.

"We should've asked your mother more questions. She must know something."

"She's in a bad way. Best not to push it. Anyway, she'd probably tell you to go home, and ground me."

"So what are we going to do?"

"Take action, that's what. Let's go see my dad." He leapt from the bed.

"In jail? They won't let us in."

"Where's your sense of adventure? We can at least try."

Flora pulled an ice-cold drink from the fridge in Fergus's room. Fergus's progressive parents had put a small fridge in each of the bedrooms and kept them stocked full of drinks. Flora took full advantage of the contents whenever she could. She held the can to her head for a minute, pulled the tab, and slugged down the liquid. She sighed. "I'm ready. Let's do this."

They clattered down the stairs, but Fergus headed back towards the kitchen.

"Where are you going?"

"To get the keys for Murdoch's quad bike."

"What? We're not going on that. No way."

"Don't be such a wuss."

"It's against the law for you to drive it."

"I'll pretend I'm Murdoch. We're the dead spit of each other. Are you going to dob me in?"

Flora resigned herself to her fate. "Drive it slowly."

"Like *that's* gonna happen. We're on a deadline here."

As they left the house, they met one of Duncan's friends.

"Uncle Gerunt, have you heard what happened? They've arrested Dad."

"Rad phoned me with the news. I came straight over."

"She's in her studio. Bye now."

"He's got no hair," said Flora, looking behind her.

"Shush, he'll hear you. He's always been like that."

"I mean like *no* hair. None at all. Not even his eyebrows and eyelashes."

"He's got some rare condition. Alopecia Universal or something. It's longer than that but we've not got time for talking about medical conditions."

"That is so weird."

"His kids have it as well. It's just them. We're all used to it. Now come on."

"Is it in any other branch of your family? Could your kids get it?"

"We're not really related, he's my dad's pal. Been around forever."

"Hard to tell with your family. You seem to have squillions of relatives."

"It's not that big." Fergus wasn't waiting around to have any more of this conversation. He was heading for the door and the quad bike.

Chapter 6

Fergus chucked Flora a helmet and leather jacket. "Put these on."

Flora held the outfit without making a move to put it on.

"Are you allowed to use this on the road?" She was still standing about three feet from the bright red bike. *Jeez, I've seen fire engines smaller than this.*

"Murdoch is. He's also allowed to take passengers."

They donned their gear and even Fergus put on trousers.

"That's the first time I've seen you in anything but shorts."

"Needs must. No need to draw any unwanted attention."

Flora threw her leg over the leather seat and sat down. She rested her feet squarely on the footplates. Fergus hopped on the front. She grasped the grab bar on either side of her tightly.

"This is not my idea of a fun day out."

"For someone so adventurous, you can be a right big girl's blouse."

"Rack off, Fergus. I'm not such a scaredy cat I couldn't take you on in a fist fight any day."

"Ooh. Hark at you."

Fergus switched on the ignition and pulled in the clutch lever. As he pressed the shifter down four times with his foot, Flora's knuckles were white. A press of the ignition and the engine roared into life. They moved forward slowly at first and then faster.

Fergus drove quickly down the steep hill towards Queen Street. It was then a straight road into town, and they picked up speed. Flora felt sick with the smell of diesel fumes. A motorbike passed them, revving its engine. Flora, startled, moved slightly and her foot slipped off the bike. In her panic she imagined it being ripped off in a combination of tarmac and speed. She yanked it back from the jaws of doom and placed it firmly on the footrest. She was sure she could hear the thundering of her heartbeat above the roar of the bike.

As the journey continued without incident, she started to relax and take in her surroundings. The River Tay was looking bonnie in the sunlight. *Most people my age would be down the beach getting a sun tan, not chasing thieves. Seriously. How do I get myself into these things?*

Fergus parked outside the *Discovery*, a historic ship down by the waterfront. Nowhere near a police station so no one to ask awkward questions about the bike. He hopped off, removed his helmet and looked at his watch. No-nonsense black, just like his clothes, it was an early birthday present from his dad. A tsunami of grief threatened to sweep him away. He swallowed against the fear that had tightened his throat. "Let's go. It's seven minutes past ten." He set off at a fair lick, his canvas shoes pounding on the cracked pavements. Shoppers jumped aside as he threatened to mow them down.

"Watch what you're doing."

"Idiots."

"Kids today."

Fergus ignored them and continued the manic pace, leaving Flora gasping behind him.

"Oi, Superman, slow down."

"Can't. We've got to rescue my dad. No time for hurry up and wait."

Fergus didn't break his pace, or his breath, until they reached Bell Street Station. Flora, red faced, was about three minutes behind him. She leaned over, hands on knees, and gagged. "Are you trying to kill me?"

"I'm the one with asthma. You're just a knacker."

"You are so dead."

Chapter 7

W hat makes you think I'm letting you in to see a prisoner? You're a couple of bairns. Go home to your mothers."

Fergus and Flora stared at a mountain in a uniform. Like the mountain, he was apparently immovable.

"Please. You've got to let me see him." Fergus's voice had an unmistakable tremble. That lump was back in his throat and no amount of swallowing was going to move it this time.

Flora had had enough of this. She was the star of the school Am Dram, and she decided it was time to put her acting skills to the test. She burst into racking sobs and even managed to force out a few tears. Seeing Fergus so upset was making her a bit emotional anyway.

"P-p-p-please. Let me see him. He's like an u-u-uncle. I'm so scared. I've gotta see he's okay. Just for a few minutes. Please. We'll be good."

The mountain melted and was now looking more like a bonny wee hill.

"Och, lassie. Dinnae get yourself worked up. I'll see what I can do. Take a seat and make yourself comfy." He turned and walked through a door.

Flora wasn't sure if there was a CCTV camera so she kept up the act.

"What's with the waterworks?" Fergus whispered.

Flora ignored him and carried on sobbing. She believed her Oscar would follow shortly.

Not only did they get to see Fergus's dad but they did so in a cosy office.

Flora gazed around the room, taking in the photos and the book-clad walls. "It's a bit small. I thought we'd be in a horrible interview room, all peeling paint and cameras."

Duncan ignored her and spoke to Fergus. "What are you doing here?"

Fergus reddened under his father's glare. He knew that look and it wasn't good. He was in serious trouble.

"We—"

Flora turned her gaze from the book-lined walls towards Duncan. "We're here to free you from your incarceration. We're not leaving you here to rot."

"I was talking to my son."

"Why do they think you did it?" asked Fergus.

"You are not to get involved. This is none of your business."

"My dad's in jail. How can that not be my business? Why do they think it was you?" Fergus could feel his chest tighten and pulled out his inhaler. Taking a couple of puffs, he recapped it and shoved it deep in his pocket. He hadn't needed it for months, but habit meant he always had it on him. He clasped his hands together to still the shaking.

"You don't need to know."

"We've come all the way down here. You might as well tell me." He held his father's gaze. Duncan dropped his eyes first.

"I'm the only member of the archaeological team who has a key to the museum." His voice was steady but the tic just above his right eye gave testament to his deeper feelings.

"It could've been Mum, or me, or any one of your trillion other sons."

"Don't be so daft. You're not helping, Fergus. Keep out of it."

"They must have something else on you. What about Ahmed? He's come over from Egypt for the tour."

"Leave this alone, Fergus. I'm serious. This family is in enough trouble."

"We would've baked you a cake with a file in it, but we didn't have time," said Flora.

Duncan cracked the first smile they'd seen. "You need to stop watching bad movies, young lady."

"We'll get you out."

"How did you pair get in here?"

"Ask Mata Hari here." Fergus waved a hand in Flora's general direction. "She put on a display the sergeant fell for hook, line and sinker."

The sergeant in question returned just like a genie from a lamp.

"You pair need to leave. The detective who owns this office is on her way back. She'll lock you up and throw away the key."

Chapter 8

Fergus bought a couple of ice creams and they licked them as they hurried back to the *Discovery*.

"It's as hot as hell. Where's this weather come from?" asked Flora.

"Your mother would ground you for a decade if she heard you using language like that."

"My mother's not here. What's she gonna do about it? Anyway, she doesn't mind me calling Bella 'Hell's Bells'."

"To answer your question, the weather's come from Russia."

"You are so weird. What should we do now, Sherlock?"

"We're going to find Ahmed."

They leapt on the bike. Fergus revved it up and they were off at full throttle. Flora held on as though her life depended on it. Mainly because she thought it did.

Ahmed was staying in the Apex Hotel down at the docks. Fergus parked up as close as he could. "Got any change for parking?" Between them they rustled up the right change for the machine, and he slapped the ticket on the front of the bike. Not sure if he needed one, he wasn't about to take any chances.

"Al Capone, that Mafia chap, was caught because he didn't pay his taxes," he informed Flora.

"What's that got to do with anything?"

"'Cause I don't want to get caught for not paying my parking."

"Seriously, you know some weird crap."

"Yep."

"Why isn't Ahmed staying with you lot if he's such good friends with your father? You must have about a million spare bedrooms."

"Heaps. I've no clue why he wanted to stay here. It's a bit posh, though."

They approached the reception desk and asked for Ahmed. The woman at the desk looked them up and down without saying a word, then picked up the phone. He wasn't in.

"Come on. If I know Ahmed, he'll be somewhere with a bit of history." Fergus patted his pocket to make sure he still had his inhaler and then jogged along the dock.

"You've got to be kidding." Flora set off after him.

He paused at the entrance to HM Frigate *Unicorn* and took a quick look around. The two-hundred-year-old ship floated proudly in the water of the modern dock. Against a background of newly built houses and flats it should have looked out of place. Yet it didn't. It hadn't seen military service since the 1960s but now did sterling service as a tourist attraction. Fergus was sure that Ahmed would gravitate towards this, the nearest thing to an archaeological site he could find. He thundered up the gangplank, his lanky legs taking the ridges three at a time.

Flora hurried after him, tripped over the first ridge and performed an ungainly pirouette before crashing to the ground. She called to Fergus but he had disappeared through the door in the ancient wooden bulkhead. She could hear the beating of his feet on the deck.

"Leave me, why don't you," she muttered, clambering up. She dusted herself off and limped for dramatic effect when she saw Fergus.

It was wasted on him, as he wasn't paying her a blind bit of notice. In fact he was intent on rummaging in his pockets. He pulled out a fiver and said, "Got any dosh? There's an entry fee."

Flora had twenty quid but wasn't keen on handing it over to the dishy bloke on the door. She thought she'd try to get a freebie. The limp became more pronounced and her lip trembled. She was trying for bravado with a hint of pathos, and carried it off with aplomb. "I almost broke my neck coming in here. My ankle's killing me." The ferocity of the lip trembling increased.

Dishy took the hint that free entry would solve the issue and hurried them through. Flora winked at Fergus and hobbled on board. Angelina Jolie could take lessons.

"Fergus, why have you dragged me here? What's this place got to do with anything?"

"It's the closest ancient monument to the hotel. It would be like a magnet to Ahmed."

"I still don't get it. What are we going to do if we find him?"

"If we find him, we speak to him. If not, I have an idea. When I was in Egypt, Ahmed used to leave messages for his son in strange places. His son would have to find them. He might be doing the same here."

"Don't you think that's a bit of a weird jump?"

"Humour me. It's all we've got."

"There're about twenty million ancient monuments in Dundee. We could be wandering around until school starts again."

The ship swayed gently on the water as they searched it from port to starboard, bow to stern. The Egyptian was nowhere to be seen. They moved, quickly at first, through the hatches between decks.

"Look." Fergus pointed at the steps.

"I can't see a thing."

"Wait here."

Fergus dashed up the stairs and grabbed one of the many lanterns that were available. Originally supplied for a kids' pirate event the crew had been running, the lanterns had been left for the general public to use in the darker places aboard ship.

He returned to Flora and pointed at some wet footsteps. "Someone's been down in the bilges."

"Oh, what a revelation. It'll be one of the crew."

"Probably, but we're going down there anyway."

Giving in to the inevitable, Flora decided to go with the plan, however stupid it seemed. Fergus was easy-going but could be the most stubborn lad on the planet when he got an idea into his noggin. Flora grasped the ropes, as the ladderways narrowed and steepened, anxious not to repeat her fall. As they reached the bilges, the stench of stale water hit them like a football at full force. Fergus, bent double in deference to his height, led the way along the walkways to the side. He held his nose and breathed through his mouth.

"Do we need to do this?" asked Flora. "Surely we'd see him." Even she had to stoop to avoid battering her head on the overhead. She stopped. Screamed. "A rat. I've just seen a *rat*."

"It'll be a dummy, dummy. For effect."

"I don't think so, smartie. Not unless they've dummies that run around," Flora retorted indignantly.

"What?" He took a couple of puffs of his inhaler and carried on.

"You are joking." She rolled her eyes. *What did* he *have to get stressed about?* He *didn't see the rat!*

Fergus ignored her.

"Seriously. Ignore me, why don't you? What on earth do you think you're going to find here anyway?"

"Call it a hunch, intuition, whatever. Just humour me."

Despite her fear, Flora forced one foot in front of the other and followed.

Fergus peered through the rails at the bilge water. This had more to do with moving his neck to get rid of a crick than intense detecting. But then he caught a vague glint.

"Look. Down there. What's that?"

"That lantern's not exactly ten million watt. I can't see a thing."

"You need specs." He grinned to take the sting from his words. Whipping out his phone, he powered up the flashlight and pointed it at the water. There was something glistening.

Flora peered at it. "Looks like a gold chain."

"I'm going down."

"That's crazy. You'll never get up again."

He removed his belt and instructed her to do the same.

"I never thought I'd be stripping in a battleship."

"Ha, flaming ha. I'm going to buckle them together. You can pull me back up."

"That ain't gonna happen. I'm lightest; I'll go down."

Fergus chewed his lip and then handed her the end of the belt. "Hold on tight. There might be rats in the water."

"*Rats?* No way I'm going down there if there's rats!"

"I was kidding. I don't think there are many water rats in Dundee. Not on a wee ship like this, anyway."

Why does crap like this always happen when I'm with Fergus. Resigning herself to her fate, she took a deep breath. She instantly regretted it, given the rancid smell, but grasped the belt. She sat down on the walkway and slipped over the edge. She tried to breathe in and out through her mouth to avoid the stink of the water. She couldn't quite reach the chain so edged further. She slipped and ended up in the filthy water. She yanked the chain from the fetid liquid and shoved it in her pocket. *All I need to do now is lose the damn thing again. Not that I think it's got anything to do with the case but better not take any chances.* She grasped the belt like a lifeline. "Get me out. Now."

Two of the crew appeared, alerted by the noise.

"What are you pair up to?"

Fergus yanked Flora out of the water and they scuttled off as fast as their bent bodies would allow. The crew were much more proficient in navigating the ship. They took off in hot pursuit but were slower than usual due to the water which Flora was liberally dripping over the deck. The stairs proved to be Flora's undoing. The rubber soles of her shoes slipped and she fell back, her bottom landing on the deck with a slap. Fergus slowed to see what had happened and the pair were captured.

They were both frog-marched to the top deck. The bulkheads shook with the voice of the Captain ticking them off.

"How dare you act like this on my ship. After two hundred years, she deserves to be treated with respect. Not have a pair of hooligans like you running around."

"Sorry."

Their apologies had little effect in calming the irate Captain. They were thrown off the ship and ordered never to return.

"Good job we didn't want to join the Navy, then," said Fergus as they walked back along the dock.

Flora, squelching along beside him, said, "I wouldn't join the Navy for a million quid. My clothes are ruined."

Chapter 9

Flora was dumped off the quad bike at her house.

"You stink. Get sorted and I'll be back later."

"Don't thank me or anything. I was helping you."

"Murdoch is going to bury me when he sees his bike. You've made a right old mess with your mucky clothes. I'm off to clean it."

"Where is Murdoch anyway?"

"He's been away helping at some sort of kids' camp. He's back tomorrow. He's not using the quad much these days, so hopefully he might not notice."

"Yeah, right. He'll bury you."

She trailed up the stairs leaving black footprints over the cream coloured carpet. *Short of teleporting, there's not a lot I can do about it.*

As she was coming out from the shower, she heard her mother screeching.

"Flora MacDonald, get your lazy backside down here."

Lazy, thought Flora. *That's rich coming from someone whose idea of exercise is pouring whisky into a glass and lifting it to her perfectly lipsticked lips.*

"I mean it. Get down here or I'll kill you."

"Pipe down; I'm coming. You'll frighten Bella."

She wrapped the bath towel round her tightly and trudged down the stairs. Her look could have curdled ice cream.

"What is it now?"

"Treat me with respect, young lady. I'm your mother." Sarah MacDonald stood with her hands on her hips, her green eyes hard and cold as she glared at Flora. With her bushy blonde hair and huge bosom resting on the shelf of her crossed arms, she resembled a mama gorilla scolding her troop.

"Fine. What've I done?" Flora refused to be cowed.

"What have you done?" Sarah pointed at the black footprints.

"I'm fine. Thanks for asking. Surprising, considering I fell into filthy water."

Bella, who was hovering in the playroom doorway started to whimper. Flora moved over and put her arm around her.

"Hey, Hell's Bells, what's wrong?"

The nickname made Bella smile but didn't divert her. "You got hurt. Are you okay?"

"Good as golden nuggets, sis. The only thing that's hurt is the carpet."

"You're silly, Flora. I can help you clean the carpet."

Their mother shifted impatiently throughout this exchange. Her fists were clenched as though she were considering assault and battery. Not that she'd ever hurt either of them, but Flora wasn't taking any chances. She stepped in front of Bella just in case.

"No, you won't, Bella," said Sarah, her tone softening slightly. "It isn't *your* problem. Your sister can get the worst of it off herself. The cleaner will finish it properly when she comes tomorrow. As for you, Flora, I will think of a suitable punishment since grounding seems to have no effect."

I'll ignore that one as well, you miserable old cow. Flora stomped off and switched on the radio while she got dressed. Singing along to one of her favourite songs cheered her up. At the end the DJ didn't have time to utter even one syllable before a newsflash cut in.

Breaking News—Is the Dagger's Curse actually real? This is the question being asked after the curse apparently claimed its first victim in Dundee. Jacob

Lieberman, a sixteen-year-old pupil at Gracemore Academy, has died under mysterious circumstances. The boy recently posted on Twitter:

#Dagger'sCurse. Wicked. Bring it on. #Can'tGetMe.

The teenager was found dead in his room this morning. The police have not released details as to the possible cause of his death. Further updates will be given throughout the day.

Flora had no sooner donned some clean clothes than her phone started beeping. Grabbing it, she glanced at the screen and answered.

"Hey, Fergus!"

"Flora, have you got the radio on?" Fergus's voice was loud.

"Sure have. What was that all about?"

"This isn't funny. It looks like the curse is real."

"Too right it's real. That's why we've got to solve this pronto. I'm on my way."

She hung up, applied a smidgeon of mascara, bolted down the stairs and out of the door before her mother could see her. She then nicked her mother's bike, hers being still at Fergus's, and set off at top speed in the direction of Broughty Ferry. She pounded the pedals like the Daemons of the curse were in hot pursuit.

Chapter 10

Flora let herself into Fergus's house and rushed up to his room. She crashed through the door. "How lucky are you to live in the one place in the house we can sleuth without an adult in sight. No one to peer over our shoulders."

"It's freaking awesome," Fergus agreed. "I'm luckier than the luckiest person alive. Don't feel particularly lucky at the moment though."

"S'pose not. That gold chain any help?"

"It's a cartouche."

"It's a what?"

"A cartouche. A small pendant with an inscription."

"Let's see it then."

He'd popped it in a cloth bag for protection. He pulled it out, applied a tiny amount of liquid from a huge bottle and rubbed it with a cloth. A few faint symbols appeared.

"Is that hieroglyphics?"

"Looks like." Fergus carried on with the cleaning.

"What's it say?"

Fergus peered at the symbols. "It's a bit difficult to see. Looks like a feather and a man."

Flora leaned in. "Is that a snake?"

"Could be." He pulled out his phone and opened an app. "I think that means 'father'."

"Okay. What's the next word?"

"I know that one. It's a half moon. That means 'of'."

"'Father of …' What, though?"

"It looks like 'free'."

"That makes no sense."

"Could be 'father of freedom' or 'father of the free'."

"Do you think it's Ahmed's?"

"I've seen him wearing something like this, so it could be. Not many people roam around Dundee with these round their necks."

"Do you think he stole the dagger?"

"Just because he wears a cartouche doesn't mean he's a thief."

"Think about it. What do we know?"

"Not much."

"Stop being such a sook. We know more than we did yesterday."

"Which gets us nowhere."

They wrote everything down on a large sketching pad. They knew that HM Frigate *Unicorn* was somehow involved. It looked as though Ahmed had something to do with the whole sorry affair. From the cartouche, it sounded as if he could be involved in some sort of freedom movement. That was about the sum of it.

Fergus, having inherited artistic talent from his mother, drew the hieroglyphs on a separate sheet. This done, it was time for more action. Rampaging through ships was more their thing. It smacked of swashbuckling, much more exciting than sitting around looking at hieroglyphics. During the summer holidays, anyway.

"We need to be doing if we're goin' to get my dad out of prison."

"Righty ho. Let's have at it. At what, though?"

"Ahmed's our man. As it's the afternoon, he'll have gone back to the hotel for a wee nap. No one from the Middle East works during the afternoon. It's too hot."

"They seem like wise people to me."

Chapter 11

Dogged pursuit became their watchword. A different, but equally snooty, reception clerk gave them the evil eye. Flora had an overwhelming urge to kick the woman in the shins. She resisted for the sake of the investigation. Also, she wasn't keen to join Duncan in prison. *I hope the curse gets you,* she thought.

"How do you know Mr Minkah?"

"He's a friend of my family," said Fergus. Then for good measure, "For, like, forever." He was hoping that would seal the deal and it did. Miss Snooty phoned through to Ahmed's suite. Result.

Within a few minutes a tall man wearing a suit and red-and-white keffiyeh approached them.

"MarHaban, Master Fergus." He kissed Fergus on both cheeks.

"MarHaban, Ahmed," Fergus responded with the traditional greeting. It was one of the few Arabic phrases he knew.

"Who is the young woman? Is this your girlfriend?"

Heat spread up Fergus face. He rubbed his neck as if it were a cooling mechanism. "This is my friend, Flora."

His gaze swept Flora head to toe. "You are beautiful young lady, ma sa allah."

He extended his hand and Flora shook it formally and said, "A pleasure to meet you, Mr Minkah."

She was secretly thinking, *He's a bit creepy. Imagine saying that to a girl my age! Are these boring formalities ever going to end?*

We need to interrogate him. The answer to this was no, as it was obligatory in Arab culture to order coffee first. Flora choked down the bitter brew while beating a tattoo on the tiles with her foot.

Fergus was taking it all in his stride. His father had taught him the formalities before he'd joined him on a dig in Egypt. He sipped the coffee and made small talk with the Egyptian. Eventually he said, "You heard about my father?"

The man's face changed. "A most unfortunate incident." This was the Arabic equivalent of 'it's a complete catastrophe'.

"That dagger's worth a fortune. Doesn't it bother you it's missing?"

"It bothers me a million times. That antiquity is worth more than money to my country."

"What about the curse? Do you believe it?"

His brown eyes narrowed, transforming his face into that of a daemon. "Of course. Only fools would not!"

"You know my dad had nothing to do with this." Fergus's eyes darkened as he thought of his father in prison.

"I would like to believe you. I am saddened my old friend has betrayed me. The facts are clear, Master Fergus."

"Just exactly what facts are clear?" Fergus barely paused to draw breath before adding, "They don't seem very clear to me."

"Do not be cheeky to your elders, young man. You will treat me with respect."

Fergus swallowed hard against the angry lump in his throat and said, "Sorry, Ahmed. Please, why did they think Dad did it?"

"Your father, my esteemed colleague, was the only person with a key. His fingerprints were all over the display cabinet."

"The whole of Dundee's fingerprints would be all over the case. It's a public museum." Flora just couldn't help herself.

"I will excuse your rudeness this once." Ahmed's piercing glance focused on Flora. His eyebrows leapt to attention like a pair of Sergeant Majors on parade. "This would, in fact, be true. However, only one person with authority had their fingerprints on that case."

"How come the police told you all this? They're not exactly putting ads on social media about it."

"That is quite enough, young lady. To answer your question, it was Duncan who gave me the details. It was imperative I speak to my esteemed friend and get the story from him. It was only right I allow him to explain."

"Can you tell us anything about the dagger, Ahmed?" asked Fergus.

"There is nothing to tell other than it is gone."

"You've got to give us something. Anything that would help us work out why Dad would do this. Not that I'm saying he did, right."

"It is not my place to say. This is a family matter. I will only say you were right when you said the dagger was worth much money. To my country it is more than wealth. Your father has stolen our heritage."

"Why were you visiting the *Unicorn?*" asked Fergus.

"How do you know this?"

Fergus opened his mouth but Flora swiftly intervened. "We asked. They said a distinguished Arabic gentleman had visited."

"I am an archaeologist. A historian. I was interested in seeing your national treasures."

"Thank you, Mr Minkah." Flora dragged Fergus off before he could say anything else.

She waited until they were further down the corridor before saying, "National treasures? Not likely, Watson. He's right up to the top of his Egyptian headdress in dastardly deeds."

"We hadn't finished with him," said Fergus.

"No, we hadn't. But we're not letting on that we're on to him."

"You've got hidden depths, Flora MacDonald. Maybe you're the spit of your great, great, multiplied grandmother after all."

Chapter 12

They decided another trip to the *Unicorn* was needed. In the absence of anything concrete to go on, it was their only hope. Plus they hadn't quite finished searching before they were told to sling their hook.

When they got there, it turned out the ban was still in place. A couple of phone calls and reinforcements in the form of two boys from school were drafted in. Bek Slater and Nathan Black would visit the ship the next day and inspect every inch of the bilge deck. Wee Nathan would be able to reach the parts other kids could not. There might be something further that they had missed.

"For heaven's sake, don't cause a stramash," warned Fergus. "They'll ban every teen and kid in Dundee."

"That's rich coming from someone who was chucked off today," said Bek.

Armed with instructions on where to scrutinise and what to look for, they promised to behave.

Fergus and Flora needed to work out what Ahmed had been examining so intently that he didn't notice the cartouche being torn from his neck. The boys' sortie would hopefully give them the answers.

"In the meantime," said Flora, turning to Fergus, "there's a party down Broughty Ferry Beach. Shall we go?"

"We're in the middle of an investigation. We can't go party."

"Even Sherlock Holmes stopped for an opium pipe. I'm sure it'll be all right if we eat a burger."

"I'm not sure that's much of an example." Fergus shoved a lock of his curly black hair back from his eyes and his beaming smile appeared. "Let's do this. They're not gonna let my dad out tonight anyhow. Ready to party?"

"Totes."

Given it was the beach, the party was more dress down than dress up. The smell of barbecue mingled with the cloying scent of perfume and the sea air. It was a pungent mix, which, added to the music and the sun, acted like a drug. The party-goers were in and out of the water, and screams and laughter filled the air. As the party progressed, the sounds grew shrill. The type of sound that sets eardrums on fire and makes adults reach for the whisky bottle.

Flora was leaning on one arm on the sand and using the other to devour a burger. A fried onion hung precariously for a few seconds and then gave in to gravity and dropped onto her cleavage. Leaping up, she wiped it away. She laughed as Fergus parodied her actions.

"*You* try eating a burger in that position."

"Nah. You're okay. I can't get over your love affair with dead cow."

"Go foist your beliefs on someone else. I like meat. Get over it."

Stace McIntyre shimmied up to them, her huge bum jiggling. From her stance it was obvious she'd been drinking.

"What do *you* want?" Flora's voice dropped a few degrees in temperature.

"Hi, Stace. What can we do for you?" In usual Fergus fashion, he flashed the girl a smile that melted the heart of every girl present. Apart from Stace.

"You pair are like an old married couple. Never apart."

"Jealous, are you?" Flora shot back.

"Of you? No way."

"Get lost, Stace. No one here cares about you. Go back

to your acolytes before I slap you in the face," said Flora.

"At least my best friend's dad didn't steal a priceless dagger."

Flora grabbed Fergus by the arm to stop him leaping up. She needn't have bothered as he didn't move a muscle.

Stace marched off as fast as sand would allow.

"Stupid cow," Flora muttered. "Why can't the curse take *her*? If it doesn't, I'll kill her myself."

"Don't be so nasty. Not everyone can be as awesome as us." Despite his words, Fergus looked miserable.

They stayed for a couple of hours. Of course all the talk was about the dagger. On the bright side there was more dancing, eating and shrieking than talking. Fergus was able to forget his troubles for a wee while.

They left when the older kids cracked open the alcohol. They really would be grounded for life if they started that caper. That couldn't happen. They'd an investigation to carry out.

Chapter 13

The next morning brought news of another kind. Flora grabbed her phone, as vital as her limbs, as soon as she opened her eyes and checked her accounts for any activity. Everywhere was awash with the news: Stace McIntyre, last seen snogging Darren on the beach, was missing. Tegan thought she was just being a drama queen and hanging out somewhere. Stace's besties were distraught, saying she wouldn't disappear without letting them know. All parentals were being rung to find out if she'd stayed over. The police were involved and an all-out search was underway. Scottish Television was also putting out an appeal for information. Social media was the fount of all knowledge and had pulled out all the stops in this case. One poster, known only as Cool Dude, put into words what they were all thinking: Stace McIntyre had been taken by the curse.

As Flora read the news, waves of sickness rolled over her. She leapt from the bed, ran to the toilet and threw up violently. Shaking, she wiped a cloth over her face and brushed her teeth. *This is my fault. I brought the curse on her. What am I going to do? If she's dead, they'll arrest me.*

Hands still shaking, she made several attempts to get dressed. The resulting outfit was a vision in pink and purple. She completed the ensemble with yellow running shoes. She leapt on her bike, and adrenalin gave her superhuman power. so that her ride to Broughty Ferry and Fergus's house took less than ten minutes.

Flora clattered through the front door and banged into

Rad, who had made an effort to clean herself up but still looked like a multi-hued ghost.

"Fergus is making breakfast. Are you okay? You don't look so good."

With a non-committal nod, Flora hurried through to the kitchen. Fergus had dark rings under his eyes that could have rivalled those on Jupiter, Saturn or Uranus. He was half nodding off over a bowl of cardboard masquerading as cereal.

Flora said, "You look like someone's smacked you in the face with a chip pan."

"I feel like it. About twenty-seven seconds sleep has that effect."

"Never mind your sleep. Stace has gone missing."

"What?"

"Have you not been on online?"

"My phone's in intensive care. Dropped it in the sea last night."

"You are seriously useless when it comes to phones. Crank open your computer. We'll look there." She dragged him through to the lounge where a communal computer resided.

Dundee was buzzing with the news. Actually, with gossip. Genuine news was a bit thin on the ground. The kindest versions of the tales indicated that Stace could have stolen the dagger and absconded with it.

"Yeah, right," said Flora. "She's as thick as a clootie dumpling. She couldn't steal a donut from a paper bag." Despite her flippant words, her face was the colour of cold porridge.

"Not even if the paper bag was torn. Better be nice about her, though. Whatever's happened it doesn't sound good."

The cruellest versions said she'd been kidnapped or murdered. All were in agreement that the curse was involved. The citizens of Dundee had been told that the consequences of messing with the dagger would be an unleashing of evil. They were now beginning to believe it. The chatter on the airwaves had an anxious edge. It wouldn't take a lot to tip it over to hysteria.

"You're right, Fergus. Even Stace didn't deserve whatever has happened to her. I'm crossing everything I possess that she's found safe and sound."

She did just that. Fergus mirrored her actions.

"She will be found, won't she?"

Fergus was at a loss for reassuring words so just kept quiet.

Flora joined him in silence for a few seconds but couldn't keep it up for long. "What're you gonna do about your phone?"

"I'll get a new one. We've more money than the Royal Bank of Scotland."

"I've been thinking about that. That dagger's worth a fortune. Do you think your dad needed the money?"

"Nah. They've been splashing the cash as much as usual."

"Maybe that's the problem. They've spent it all. Do you think your mum'll tell us?"

"No chance. 'Sides, you're not right."

Flora metaphorically rolled up her sleeves. "Lead me to your dad's computer."

"You'll end up in jail yourself!"

"Nah. Not with my acting skills. Come on. We haven't got time to waste."

The computer was harder to crack than she thought. Fergus gave her a list of likely passwords and left her to it. All failed. She even tried Dagger's Curse. No joy. "I need a Coke," she yelled through the half open door. Her willing slave obliged. She took a long gulp and sighed. *Good job I want to be an archaeologist. No way I'm going into computers.*

"Have you got no clue?" she said.

"Nope. He changes it nearly every week."

She had a brainwave. "What was the name of the King when the dagger was made?"

"Our King? How the heck do I know?"

"No, you dozy pillock. The Egyptian king."

"Can't remember. They gave us a sheet at the museum. I'll find it."

When he returned, she was banging her head on the desk.

"You're so dramatic. It was Mentuhotep the First."

Flora tried Mentuhotep1—no joy. Fergus sank into a chair. She tried MentuhotepI—nothing. Mentuh0tep1—bingo, she was in.

"Easy, peasy. Now let's have a look at the files."

The files were also locked down, but she cracked them in seconds. This involved adding the first and last password together to make one new password and then so on down and up the list.

"Were you a safe cracker in a former life, or something?"

"Something like that."

One file had the title of accounts. A quick double click and they both stared at the screen. It took a few seconds for them to take in the information.

"You're father's broke."

"He can't be. We've pots of money."

"Not according to this, you've not."

After searching every file on the computer, they were no further forward.

"Can you get into his bank account?" asked Fergus.

"No way. That's taking it too far. I'm not getting arrested for real."

They snagged a couple of chocolate bars and took them into the garden. Flora sat in the leafy shade of a huge tree. The bark was cool through her top. Flora looked up at the names they'd engraved in the bark many years ago.

"Do you remember the day we climbed the tree and carved our initials there?"

Fergus looked up at the scratches. "Remember! How could I forget since you ended up in Casualty with a broken arm, and I ended up grounded for days."

Flora chuckled and bit into the chocolate bar. Bliss.

Fergus paced around the garden, Hatshepsut the dachshund nipping at his heels. Despite her size, the dog lived up to her name: she ruled with an iron paw and everyone did her bidding.

"Are you going to eat that sweet or just squeeze it?"

Fergus stared at the mangled mess in his hand. The puzzlement on his face was painful to watch. He licked his hands. Wiped them on his shorts. Looked up at Flora and shrugged.

"What are we going to do?" He swallowed, and then shook his head, making his curly hair even wilder. "I think he might have done it."

"Rubbish. Your dad's the honestest dude on the planet."

"That's not a word."

"I know. What are you, the word police? I think I might have put the curse on Stace."

"You talk a load of crap at times. You can't control the curse."

"You sure?"

"Positive. My dad's the master of curses." He stopped. The shadows under his eyes gave him a haunted look. "He might also be a master criminal."

"You say *I* talk crap. Get a hold of yourself. You're worse than Watson."

Flora's phone rang. She glanced at the screen and answered, "'S up?" She listened to the garbled voice. "Maccie D's, twenty minutes. Got it."

As she thumbed off the phone, Fergus was already pulling the quad bike keys from his pocket.

Chapter 14

Bek and Nathan were chomping their way through Big Macs and fries. Flora had some notes she'd liberated from her mother's purse. She bought a large fries for herself and a spicy beanburger for her partner in crime. A couple of chocolate milkshakes joined them on the tray. Holmes and Watson didn't work on an empty stomach. Neither would she. Suitably fortified, they were ready for the update.

"Jeez, Flora. What are you wearing? Are you colour blind?" said Nathan, his eyes wide with wonder.

"Never mind my clothes. What've you got?"

"That place stinks," said Bek. "You owe us."

"You'll like what we found though," added Nathan. His grin was the size of Scotland and his eyes shone with excitement.

They handed over a grubby sheet of paper that contained a complex drawing.

"Sorry about the dirt. It's filthy down there," said Bek.

"Tell me about it." Flora shuddered at her flashbacks.

Fergus grabbed the paper and peered at it. His eyes brightened for the first time that day as he recognised some of the scrawled figures on the bottom half of the page. He tapped his forefinger on a diagram at the top.

"That looks like the front of the bilge deck. Or the bow to be precise."

"Don't know 'bout that," said Nathan. "It was a tight squeeze, though."

"What's that wee diagram under it?" said Fergus. "And a number. Your writing's rubbish."

"You try drawing in a tiny space on a dirty boat. It says 'hidden compartment'."

"He had to use his pen knife to force it open," added Bek.

"God spare us. We'll all be locked up for vandalism," said Flora. "Was there anything in it?"

"Some fluff."

"That's hardly momentous. Why have a secret compartment with nothing but a bit of fluff in it? Holmes and Watson didn't have to deal with that sort of stuff."

"Was it big enough to hold the dagger?" Fergus drummed his fingers on the formica table.

"No clue. I never got to see the dagger before it was nicked."

"Well, if it was, then the fluff could be from a cloth it was wrapped in."

"Well, geek, you strike again. Maybe your detecting skills are up there with Holmes after all." Flora teased her friend to hide her admiration.

Fergus wasn't listening to her. "You guys rock. Sorry, but we'll have to go." He leapt up and loped out of the restaurant.

"Hang on." Flora swallowed the remainder of her burger and grabbed her milkshake. "Where are we going?" she yelled at his retreating back.

"The library." He disappeared up the escalator, running rather than using the electrics to aid his trajectory upwards.

Seriously, how did I end up with a best friend who's a fitness freak. All this running and chasing about isn't good for me. I'm knackered.

The reference library was cool and chock full of books that would help them.

"Can't we just google it?" asked Flora.

"Not enough time on the computers. Besides, we don't want to leave a trail."

"You're getting good with the cloak and dagger stuff."

Fergus knew exactly where the books were to be found.

He spent a lot of time in the library, especially in the Ancient Egyptian collection. They found a table far away from prying eyes and dumped the books down. Fergus pulled the paper from the pocket of his shorts and slapped it on the table

The rest of the paper was covered in Nathan's hasty rendition of the hieroglyphics he had seen on the frigate.

"This will take forever," said Flora.

"I'll photocopy it. We'll do half each." He hefted a large book towards her. "Here, start boning up on your hieroglyphs."

Flora pulled the book towards her and opened it.

Chapter 15

Flora chucked her pen down. "My head's spinning. It's splitting the rocks out there, and we're stuck in a library."

"I can't make hide nor hair of lots of this. Let's go back to the *Unicorn*. I wanna check out that hidey-hole."

"Nathan's already done it to death. What'll we find?"

"I want to know if the compartment was big enough to hold the dagger. I'd like to see the hieroglyphics in situ as well."

"Ooh. Listen to you with all the posh talk. What about the ban?"

"Sod the ban. You've ten minutes until you pull off the acting role of your life."

After an Emmy-Award-winning performance, backed up by profuse apologies, just to be sure, they were back on the frigate.

"Any more nonsense and we're calling the police."

"We promise. We're just doing research." Flora waved a notebook and pen in front of a small woman in a historical uniform. They'd grabbed them from Waterstones on their way. "Last time was a mistake. Honest."

The uniformed pixie let them on board, although her look could have frozen the River Tay.

"It's heaving on here," said Flora.

"Historical re-enactments draw crowds. We'll do our best."

Where they were going was too far down and too far forward for most people. Especially since they'd be squeezing into an area that had very little public access. Mainly because getting there was a real struggle. This area of the boat was a strange mix of ancient and modern. Old bulkheads jostled alongside modern wooden struts. The low overheads meant that a dwarf would have had to bend double to scuttle along the deck. Add to this the narrowness of the walkway and you weren't talking access for all.

Make that Flora doing the squeezing. There was no way Fergus's lanky frame would fit in there no matter what contortions he pulled.

Once inside she had little space for drawing. Despite her diminutive size she was a lot bigger than wee Nathan. She manipulated her pen into a better position. She sketched for about twenty minutes then said, "I'm done for. Pass me my phone."

"Why didn't you do that in the first place? You would've saved us loads of time."

"Why didn't you mention it then, genius?"

She snapped off several pictures of the faint hieroglyphics which had been pencilled on the hull of the ship. They'd see what a twenty-seven-inch screen could do in the way of brightening them. She had a hunt round for the hidey-hole and finally spotted it well concealed behind an out-of-the-way pillar. The cavity itself looked as old as the ship, but the door appeared to be newer.

She pried it open. "Ow!"

"Wassup? You okay?"

"I'm mortally wounded here. I've got a splinter in my finger." She pulled out the small sliver and sucked the resultant spot of blood.

First aid completed, she turned her attention back to the compartment. There was nothing inside. Dust had been disturbed, so something had been in there recently. She snapped a photo for Fergus to examine at his leisure, and then, in true Nancy Drew style, she tugged a hair from her head and put it in the door.

She crawled out and groaned as she stood. "The things I do for you, Fergus. You owe me, big time." She could barely put one foot in front of the other and stumbled.

"Watch you don't end up in the water again. We'll be banned for the rest of our natural."

"Natch. Do you think I want a repeat of my swim?"

He held her arm just to make sure. He didn't want anything to happen to her.

"So, is it big enough for the dagger?"

"Yep, with a wee bit of room to spare."

"Looks like we've found a handing over point. Go Detective Duo."

"It's a good job Sherlock's dead. He'd have found his match in you."

Free of the boat, they raced along the pier back to the quad bike. The buttery yellow sun, high in a bright blue sky, bounced off the water, bathing them in golden shimmers of light. Somehow Flora managed to reach the bike first.

"Winner, winner, stovie dinner," she shouted while trying to gulp in breaths of salt and seaweed scented air. The raucous screech of seagulls could be heard as they swooped overhead in a parody of classical dance.

"It's a bit hot to be talking about stovies." Fergus pulled up beside her looking as suave as always. He hadn't broken a sweat.

Flora noticed Callum Craig walking towards them. Her heart beat a determined tattoo inside her chest, and for a moment she found it difficult to breathe. *OMG. The hottest guy in the school. No, make that Dundee. What do I look like? I'm a wreck.* She pulled her top down, smoothed her hair and dialled up the voltage on her smile.

"Hi, Callum."

The lad lifted one eyebrow and, with a minimalist twist of the lips, went on his way.

"He smiled at me. He must like me."

"He was being polite."

"He thinks I'm fat. That's what it is. He likes skinny girls."

"There's nothing of you, Flora. How can you think you're fat?"

"He might go out with me if I was thin."

"He doesn't even look at you. He likes girls with short skirts and thick makeup. Do you fit that description?"

Flora made doe eyes at Callum's retreating back. With a sigh, she pulled on trousers, jacket and helmet and threw her leg over the quad bike. Fergus mimicked her look and followed suit with the clothing. Flora thumped him on the back and he laughed. For a wee while he was just a teenager again. Not a care in the world.

Chapter 16

The minute they walked into Fergus's house, Rad, streaked with green paint, accosted the pair.

"Have either of you seen Stace?" she demanded anxiously.

"What? You mean she's still missing?" asked Flora, fear gnawing at her insides.

"If you know anything about this, you have to talk. No hiding stuff." Rad's piercing gaze bore through her son.

"I don't, Mum. Honest."

"Are you sure?"

"I'm telling the truth."

"If you hear anything, tell me straight away. I mean it." She turned to Flora. "You too."

"Cross my heart and hope to die, Rad." Her actions mimicked her words.

Rad, and the green streaks, left them to it. Flora thought a couple of daubs of yellow paint would set off the green nicely.

The Duo headed for the kitchen, Flora's thoughts running wildly.

"Do you think we should investigate her going missing as well?" she asked.

"Flora, we've enough on our plate. Let's leave that one to the police."

"I was getting to like this detective stuff." She didn't want to admit how guilty she felt at wishing the curse on Stace.

After a quick snack, it was back to the library, the books and deciphering hieroglyphics. Thanks to the Egyptian tour, the library had a huge collection of books on Ancient Egypt. They'd borrowed them from all over the UK and had the biggest collection outside the British Library. Flora could swear some of them were as old as the hieroglyphics themselves, and as dusty as an Egyptian dig. She opened one and promptly sneezed half a dozen times. This elicited a *sshh* from the direction of the service desk.

They bagged time on a computer and plugged in Flora's phone. The blown-up photos supplemented her attempt at art.

"You acquitted yourself well there, my dear Watson. Cracking photos."

"I think that's more down to the phone company than my specialist skills."

They soon had a working translation of the communication.

> The curse will be upon the Father of Lies. Cursed be this place. Those who seek will not find. Only those in the resting place know. Foolish are the persons who believe.

They both stared at the words on the paper.

"What's all this doing on a musty old frigate anyway, boy genius?'"

"I dunno. Looks like they're using it to pass messages."

"It's a bit Famous Five, innit?"

"Yep. They say men're just little boys grown tall."

"Not that tall if they can wriggle where I've just been. I still can't move my limbs." This was accompanied by an exaggerated stretching of said limbs. She stood up and paced up and down. She noticed the librarian's gaze fixed on her. Clear gestures indicated she'd better sit down, and fast. Flora obliged.

"Stop whining."

"That's rich coming from you. You could whine for Scotland. Okay. What's the message mean?"

"No freaking clue."

"You're the one with the dad in the know."

"I'm the one with the dad in prison."

"D'you think he'll know?"

"No way we're getting into that place again."

"Your mum?"

"Doubt it."

The ringing of the phone broke the impasse.

"Tegan, what you doin'? Wanna come and join us?"

"They've found Stace."

"Where was she hiding out?"

"She's dead, Flora."

"Wha … Wha …" She started shaking.

Fergus snatched the phone from her hand.

"What's up?" he said, his voice high pitched.

"Stace McIntyre's dead. She drowned."

He pressed End and stared at Flora.

Tears streaming down her face, she said, "What have I done?"

Chapter 17

The news of the missing dagger and the death of Stace McIntyre had the usually stoic Dundonians in a tailspin. Adults slammed into survival mode and several of the Detective Duo's friends were saying online that their parents were taking them away for the remainder of the summer. Fight or flight mechanisms had stepped in. There was no tangible enemy to fight. That left flight as the only option. Parents made hurried plans to move their children far from danger.

Chapter 18

They went back to Fergus's house and sat in his room drinking ice-cold Coke.

The house phone rang and Rad trailed up the tower stairs and handed it to Flora. "It's your mother."

Flora took it with some reluctance. Her grimace was weak in comparison to her usual efforts.

"Yeah?"

"I distinctly remember grounding you."

"Sorry." For once there was a hint of sincerity in her voice, a sign of how rattled she was.

"I need you to look after Bella so I can go out."

"Could you bring her here? Rad'll look after us both. I'm scared, Mum. Stace is dead."

"I suppose so." Her mother rang off without a goodbye.

Flora thought she'd got off lightly given the fact that she'd gone behind her mother's back.

"Are you really that scared?" asked Fergus.

"Terrified. Aren't you?"

"A bit, but I'm more worried about my dear old dad. That's taking the edge off the terror."

"So what are we going to do about him?" Focusing on that was a much better idea than thinking about dead school-mates.

"We're going to research the dagger and the curse. Might make sense of the cryptic message from the *Unicorn*."

Fergus nicked his brother's MacBook and handed it to Flora, then fired up his own and they both got down to work.

There was a lot of scribbling on notepads and guzzling of soft drinks. Talking was minimal, with the occasional "Aahh" or "Nice one".

Half way through, Bella appeared. She pointed towards the computer.

Flora said, "Use your earphones, Hell's Bells. We're working."

Bella pulled them from her pocket and plugged them in. She opened up her computer game. They didn't hear another murmur from her.

After about forty-five minutes Fergus straightened his back, and cracked the bones in his neck. The sound rushed to Flora's brain and went screaming down her nerve endings.

"Do you have to do that?"

"And of course you have no bad habits. Never mind that." His eyes were shining.

Not very sensitive given their mate had died, thought Flora.

"My dad's hunch was right."

"About what?"

"That dagger was made from iron which came from a meteorite."

"In King Tut's time? Are you yanking my chain?"

"It wasn't Tutankhamun; it was Mentuhotep I."

"Whatever! How would he get his hands on a lump of meteorite iron?"

"Same way we do. It fell to earth." He squinted at the screen. "They called it metal from heaven. Revered it as coming from the deities."

"Jeez. No wonder they think it's cursed."

"This isn't just a cursed dagger. It's extraterrestrially cursed. That's off the planet."

Flora managed a feeble smile. "You knew this and didn't tell me?"

"Dad suspected but needed to wait for the test results.

According to the *Guardian* newspaper the results are in. Hope they told him in prison."

"That dagger must be worth a fortune. More than a fortune. Maybe a squillion."

"Probably the rarest artefact ever dug up. My dad's gonna go down for about a billion years for this."

"We'll make sure he doesn't." Her voice lacked its usual bravado.

Some of the information they'd dragged from the bowels of the Internet they already knew. The dagger had a gold and rock crystal handle. The sheath was decorated with a water snake, the spirit of evil, darkness and destruction. He was blamed for every disaster that befell the world.

"Why didn't your dad's team leave well alone? I'd have run a million miles at the first sign of Apep."

"I'm beginning to wonder that myself. He wouldn't do that, though. Loves his job."

It was thought the dagger originally belonged to a warrior in Mentuhotep's army.

"A poisoner had it at one time, Flora."

"A cursed, extraterrestrial, poisoned dagger. You couldn't make this up."

"There's some serious ancient Egyptian excrement going on here."

"Excrement seems to be the only thing that's not associated with that dagger."

"We could die."

"The Detective Duo had better get on with solving the mystery, then. Better than gnashing our gums."

Chapter 19

The pair stared at the paper, no more enlightened than before.

The curse will be upon the Father of Lies. Cursed be this place. Those who seek will not find. Only those in the resting place know. Foolish are the persons who believe.

Paying homage to the God of Google, Fergus typed "Father of Lies" into the search engine. It turned out to be the name for the devil who, in the Book of John in the Bible, is described as the father of lies.

"Isn't John the New Testament?"

"Yep." Fergus swung side to side in the leather swivel chair. He couldn't quite manage the top swivel speed thanks to the length of his legs, but he made a valiant attempt.

"So, long after the dagger's time."

"Give the girl a prize."

She slapped him on the arm. "Less of the cheek."

He grinned. "You're so easy to wind up."

Flora threw him a look that could kill cockroaches.

Unfazed, Fergus made a note of the Bible verse, and they looked up the other references to the phrase. There were a few songs that they were able to access online, but this was a big mistake as one of them turned out to be repulsive.

"I'm all for research, but that's put me off my lunch," said

Flora. She mimicked gagging and, given her acting prowess, it was surprisingly realistic.

"You okay?" Fergus was rising from his chair.

"Course I am, you pillock."

"Moving swiftly on."

There were also a couple of books. One was a supernatural horror, the other an exposé of the establishment.

"Don't tell me we've got to read these," said Flora.

"Nah. I don't think they'll help," said Fergus. "Let's stick with the devil version and see where that takes us."

"Straight to hell via an extraterrestrial curse is where it'll take us."

"Ever the drama queen." He grabbed the paper with the message. "I'm off to photocopy this."

He returned from Duncan's office with several sheets of paper.

Flora had grabbed a Coke from the fridge and was chugging it down like a drunk at a wedding.

She belched loudly and said, "When your parents recover from penury, do you think they'd invest in air conditioning?"

"In Dundee? Are you kidding? It would only be on for about a fortnight a year."

He snatched up a pen, scored out some words, and scribbled in a substitution.

The curse will be upon the ~~Father of Lies~~ Devil.

"That makes even less sense. How can you put a curse on the devil?" asked Flora.

"He'd be the one doing the cursing."

"What about the next bit? *Cursed be this place.* Does it mean the frigate, Dundee, Scotland, the tomb the dagger was found in?"

"Any of the above. Could be Britain, if they think we've nicked the dagger for ourselves."

"Better tell Daryl that little gem. Her father can relocate her to France instead of Cornwall."

Daryl was being dragged off for the summer to get away from the curse. The skinny on the street said she wasn't happy about leaving her besties.

"Ha ha."

"I wasn't being funny."

"Yes," yelled Bella, making them both jump.

"Bella, keep it down. You'll wake the bodies in the cemetery up the road."

Bella, used to Flora and her strange turns of phrase, just laughed. "I got to level twenny-four. It's my first time, Flora, so it's 'portant."

"Go you. Maybe dial your delight down just a wee bit."

She was talking to the air as Bella had put her earphones in again and was back in the virtual world.

After long debate and much arguing, they scored out the frigate and the tomb. They both agreed Dundee and Scotland were fair game.

Flora rummaged in the fridge again. "I'm starving."

"I'll make you a sandwich. What—"

"Jam and cheese." She wasn't taking any chances she'd end up with bean paste and hummus. She could only stretch friendship so far. Fergus nudged Bella, who left her game long enough to say she fancied egg on hers. Fergus rustled up the food and they munched in silence: the Detective Duo deep in their own thoughts, Bella deep in battling baddies or whatever she was doing in her virtual world.

Fortified, they returned to their task.

Those who seek will not find.

"They're not kidding, are they?" said Fergus.

"That bit's not right. We're going to find the dagger."

Fergus had that look in his eye that said, "Yeah, right."

"And the person who stole it."

"My sister will fix it, Fergus. She's clever," Bella chipped in.

"Arabella MacDonald, you shouldn't be listening."

"My earphone fell out. Anyway, you shouldn't have secrets. Mum'll be really mad."

"Leave Mum to me. You play your game."

They couldn't even begin to imagine what the rest of the message meant. They were about to change tack when the MacDonalds' mother turned up to take them home. No amount of protesting would sway her from this. Flora was going home to serve her punishment. *Why is my mother the worst one in the universe?* she thought morosely.

Chapter 20

The minute Flora woke up, she reached for her phone. Fergus had borrowed his mother's old one so she could FaceTime him. He appeared on her screen bare chested, wild haired, and rubbing his eyes.

"It's the middle of the night."

"Don't be such a wuss. It's after nine."

"Yeah. The middle of the night."

"I bet Batman and Robin didn't worry about the time. I'm coming over."

She left via the kitchen to grab a banana on a roll. There were better things to do during school holidays than cook bacon.

She barged through his door and caught him wearing nothing but his birthday suit. "Whoops." She backed out and waited outside.

"Have you ever heard of knocking?" His voice was muffled by the thick wooden door.

"I've had an idea." She leaned in as close to the door as she could, given she had to stand on the step below, and shouted the words. Her voice battered off the wooden panels which lined the walls of the spiral staircase. *Awesome turret rooms are all very well, but not much use if you've got to have a conversation standing in the stairwell of said turret.*

"Good for you. I'd rather not hear it while I'm standing here in the scud."

"Focus, Fergus. Never mind the fact you've displayed your meat and two veg."

She leant against the wall with her hands in her pockets wondering how one teenaged boy could take so long to get dressed. Eventually the door opened and she bolted in.

"Are you going to share your brilliant idea, Sherlock?" Fergus asked

"We'll see if any other ancient artefacts have been stolen."

"That's your idea? The police will have that covered."

"They're not gonna tell us, stupid."

"You're calling me stupid. Your idea's idiotic."

"And your idea is …?"

"Fine. We'll do it."

After a couple of hours, they had listed a few possibilities within striking distance of Dundee:

Gold cow missing in Edinburgh
Bust of Tuthmosis 3 in Perth
Figure of Horus in Stirling
Figure of Isis in Aberdeen

"Are they worth nicking?" asked Flora.

"Not sure but my dad's got books that would tell us."

"Anything in common?"

"Mostly Egyptian. All the museums have Egyptian artefacts at the mo, 'cause of the Dagger tour."

"They all look pretty small to me. Suppose they'd be easy to liberate and relocate."

"Ooh, look at you with the fancy words, Miss Flora."

"You sound like Ahmed."

They trundled through to Duncan's office. Fergus pulled a couple of huge catalogues off the shelf. They landed on the desk with a bang. Anything not anchored down jumped and clattered, and Flora caught a small ornament before it crashed to the floor.

The blood had drained from Fergus face. "Well caught."

"What are you pair up to?" yelled Rad from her studio.

"Just checking some things in one of Dad's books."

"Be careful. You know the cost of the bits he's bought."

"No worries. We're watching."

He then spoke in a whisper. "That little figure you caught is probably worth about a hundred grand."

"And it's sitting on a desk. Are you lot for real?"

Ignoring her, Fergus opened the first tome. One by one he checked prices on the stolen pieces. Flora swung around on the office chair while she waited. She caught sight of an object close to her foot and brought the swinging to a grinding halt. If she broke anything, she'd be paying for the rest of her life. Her mind turned to Stace, but she didn't want to go there. She shivered at the thought of what the girl had gone through.

"I'm off to play Bella's game on your computer," she said. A spot of distraction therapy in the way of shooting baddies was needed.

A nail biting twenty-seven minutes and a tense battle later Fergus joined her.

"The prices on these could keep us in phones and designer trainers for a trillion years."

He passed her the price list.

Sacred Cow statue (Gold)	£1,500,000
Basalt bust of Tuthmosis 3	£166,000
Sandstone relief	£5,100
Figure of Horus (Bronze)	£7,800
Figure of Isis	£509,822

Flora skipped the rest and said, "That's a serious amount of cash. Worth the risk then?"

"Oh, yes!"

"Size?"

"All filchable size."

"Someone in Dundee's running a black market in stolen antiques."

"Looks like it."

Stalled again, Fergus had a brainwave. He FaceTimed Ahmed's son. Walid and he went way back. Well, four years anyway, since they were on a dig together one summer. His mate was 100% Western and yet 100% Arabic. A modern-day chameleon like many of his friends. When asked about the Father of Lies his face gave little away. Apart from a twitch at the edge of his mouth, he was his usual smiling self.

"This is not something I can discuss. It would be disrespectful. You may try looking closer to home, my friend."

"Come on, Walid. This is crucial, man."

"I will say no more. Look close to home."

He hung up. "What's he talking about?"

"I think he's saying your dad is the Father of Lies."

"My dad? The devil?" Fergus's suddenly pale face could be read like a book and clearly that book was a horror story!

"Take it easy, pal." Flora moved to the edge of her chair, ready to grab Fergus if the situation deteriorated.

A few puffs and the inhaler had its intended effect. Fergus jumped from the bed. "We're going to follow Ahmed."

"I know you think we're Nancy Drew and the Hardy Boys, but how do you plan on doing that?"

"We're going to go incognito."

"Incognito. On a quad bike? We'll stand out like haggis at a vegan convention."

"We'll use our bikes."

The Curse at Work

The dagger more than lived up to its name. The curse would protect the dagger's owner. Anyone else coming into contact with it would die. The passage of time could be measured in mere hours when the dagger claimed its first victim. Ammon's son, eight years old and wanting to prove he was a man, picked it up. That was at breakfast. Lunch brought his death. A merciful release from an agony of bleeding and diarrhoea. As Ammon prepared the boy for his journey across to the afterlife, he knew the dagger had to go. What evil had he released on the world?

He sold the dagger to an itinerant scribe. The grizzled man admired its beauty. He desired it for protection, he said. Coins changed hands and the curse passed on. The next victim was an old woman who was seduced by its grandeur. Grasping the handle, she raised it high in the air. In the process a small nick was made in her skin. The next day she was dead. None of the healer's magic could prevent this.

Down the centuries it passed through many hands. It was stolen by a Roman Centurion. The curse was swift to act: he was convicted of treason. His punishment was to be placed in a sack full of snakes and thrown into the River Nile.

The pattern continued. The dagger travelled through many continents until fate and circumstances returned it to Egypt once more. Its rarity and exquisite design led it to be buried, in an ornate tomb, with a Pharaoh who would carry it with him to the afterlife. The power of the curse was halted. It could not reach from beyond its own grave. Its job now was to protect the dead Pharaoh, both in the afterlife and in the physical realm. No harm would befall his spirit or his body while the dagger kept its silent watch.

Chapter 21

Before they tailed anyone, there was the small matter of Flora's clothes to be dealt with. Her love affair with all things bright meant she could be seen for a fifty-mile radius. Not the stuff of detective fiction. By dint of rummaging around in all the wardrobes in the house Fergus managed to deck her out in something more suitable.

"I look like an undertaker." She tugged the oversize black T-shirt.

"Stop whining. I bet Sherlock Holmes didn't whine."

"He could wear what he wanted. Anyway, Watson complained all the time."

"What's this got to do with anything?"

"You started it."

Fergus ended the argument by cramming one of his mother's funky hats on Flora's head. He shoved a baseball cap on his own to tame his wild curls. He also donned trousers rather than his customary shorts. Sunglasses completed the ensemble, although this was more to do with the sun splitting the rocks than with covert operations. A few temporary tattoos, pinched from Iona's room, and they were good to go.

"Where are your several hundred siblings anyway? They all seem to be missing."

"There are only nine of us. Stop exaggerating."

"Are you sure? Seems like way more than that to me. What have you done with the other eight?"

"Heavens to Murgatroyd, Flora. You don't half make a

fuss. You know fine well four of them are married. The others are doing big sibling things for the summer."

"What sort of big sibling things?"

Fergus, eager to get going, was gathering up money and shoving it in his pockets. "Iona is having a gap year."

"Awesome, where is she at the mo?"

"New Zealand. Least I think she is. That's where Harris has gone to join her for the university hols anyway."

"Your family is so cool."

"They're not bad. Yours is all right, too."

"What? A dad who's missing nine months of the year and a mother who's a drunk? Bella's the sanest of the lot of them."

"They keep you supplied with dosh and don't hassle you all that much."

Flora thought she'd better keep quiet about the fact that she relocated most of her cash from her mum's purse to her own pocket. Her mum gave her no help and assistance with the transaction.

As ideas go this wasn't the brightest one. They didn't even know if Ahmed was still at the hotel. Asking wasn't an option; that would attract too much attention. They sipped at mocktails in the bar, with Flora keeping half an eye on the foyer.

"This drink's not bad," said Flora.

Fergus glared at his. "This one's horrible. It's meant to be a Virgin Mary. It's virgin on poisonous."

"That was quite funny."

They memorised every cocktail on the menu and invented several of their own. Their favourite was Explorer's Delight. This would contain apple, mango, pineapple, orange and papaya juice, non-alcoholic spiced rum and a squeeze of chilli.

"That'll keep the blood pumping," said Fergus.

Flora elbowed him in the ribs. "Ahmed's appeared."

They watched until he handed his key in and strode out through the door. Leaping up, they dropped some money on the table and headed after him.

As they reached the door a Mercedes approached. Ahmed was at the wheel. They ducked back in to avoid being seen, then raced out and grabbed their bikes. Pedalling furiously, they could see the Merc three cars in front. Fergus pulled ahead as Flora panted heavily and struggled to keep up. Fergus glanced back at her. "I'll text you the location—" and he sped off into the distance. Flora slowed and caught her breath. *Seriously, how can he be fitter than me with his asthma? Life is so not fair.* It had conveniently slipped her mind that in order to be fit you needed to do some exercise. She was never one to let the facts interfere with her sense of injustice.

Flora felt her phone vibrate and squeezed the brakes hard. Too hard. The back wheel rose about a foot in the air. She executed a perfect, if involuntary, pirouette over the handlebars. Somehow she damaged nothing more than her pride.

Mill o' Mains. Go back to my house. See you later.

Her pride took another battering right alongside her sense of injustice. She turned her bike in the direction of Broughty Ferry with a murderous look in her eye. How dare he leave her out of the exciting bits? *I'll be having strong words with Mr Fergus when I next see him.*

Chapter 22

Fergus stopped his bike at the entrance of Den O' Mains. Overgrown and unkempt, the local 'beauty spot' was an eyesore. He shoved his bike inside a tangle of bushes and tall grass. He stepped back to check it was hidden. All good, so he trotted inside, keeping close to the bushes. It wouldn't do to be seen.

Ahmed made a beeline for a huge pond, thick with green scum. Weeds choked the area, catching at his feet. He grabbed a thin sapling to stop himself falling. It bent under his ample weight but he remained upright. He halted beside the information board, took out some glasses and studied it. Pulling out his phone, he snapped a couple of photos of the board and several of the surrounding area. He rubbed at the board with a wet wipe, shook his head and muttered something. He pulled out another wet wipe and rubbed with more ferocity. Then he turned on his heels and left.

From the middle of a thick bush Fergus watched everything. Why was Ahmed wandering around with wet wipes in his pocket? He didn't think it was an Egyptian thing, regardless of how hot it got out there. It wasn't as if he had kids with him. As Ahmed passed his hiding place, Fergus held his breath. He was sure that his heartbeat would be heard above the shrill singing of the birds. Crouching down, he waited ten minutes to make sure Ahmed had gone. Then he stood up and stretched aching muscles. He made a pledge to go to the gym even more than he did already. He trotted over to the board. Someone had used a thick black pen to add graffiti over the

Perspex. Or was it? It was just about possible to make out a bit of what was being said, but it made no sense. Despite Ahmed's attempt at cleaning, the words were faint but clear. Just not in any sensible order. Following Ahmed's example, Fergus took a couple of shots on his phone. Then, just in case it was important, he took a few of the surrounding area.

Chapter 23

When Flora arrived at the house of the magnificent turret, Rad was out. She ferreted around in the undergrowth for the hidden key, let herself in and snagged a Coke. Cycling was thirsty work. She decided the fully loaded sugary version was in order, given the amount of exercise she had done. She didn't have the energy for stairs, so sprawled on the sitting room sofa.

This was where Fergus found her, snoring fit to waken a host of Egyptian mummies. He poked her in the ribs. Nothing. He poured a few drops of water on her hair. She leapt up, spluttering.

"What in the name of Ramses are you doing?"

"We've work to do. You can have a kip later."

He shoved his phone under her nose.

She squinted at the screen and said, "I can't make a thing out on that screen. Fire up your laptop."

Her vra vra vroom had returned, so she bounced up the stairs to the turret two at a time. A couple of minutes and an airdrop pairing later, they were looking at the blown-up version.

Charon statue justice ship leans
Stalks bull always holds races
Father secret with small flying
of place righteous key reign
Lies kept men safe jumps

"It's not much better on here. It looks like a jumble."

"It wasn't any better in the natural."

"Is it some sort of code?"

"How would I know? I want to be an archaeologist like my dad, not a spy."

"Keep your bonnie curly black hair on. It's not *my* fault your family's in this mess."

"You'd be the same if it was your family."

"If it was my mother that was in prison I'd be rejoicing." She pumped the air several times in a triumphant gesture just to make sure her point was fully understood.

"It's obviously a code." Fergus rummaged in a drawer.

"At least it's not hieroglyphics."

"I wish it was. We'd have a fighting chance with those." He pulled out a pen and threw it over to Flora. "Let's get to work."

Armed with several freshly printed versions of the words, they got down to decoding them. Progress was slow. Sheets were scribbled on, screwed up and tossed on the floor; the computer utilised a number of times; crisp packets opened and the contents consumed. Still they were no further forward.

Fergus's rubbed his hands through his increasingly wild curls. "What've you come up with?"

"Apart from Father of Lies, nothing. 'Ship' could be a reference to the *Unicorn*."

"Could be the RRS *Discovery*. We're awash with historic ships in Dundee."

"It could be one of the cruise ships. Who the heck knows?"

"We could visit the frigate again. See if there's anything new."

"Why? What on earth new do you think will magically appear? It's a sailing ship, not a space ship."

A Taurean, Fergus could display bullish stubbornness and determination, even in the face of any evidence to the contrary.

"I still think they're using it as a drop-off point for something."

"It could be the staff using it to store hammers and things. They're doing work down there, if you hadn't noticed."

Fergus was not to be swayed and strode out of the door and down the stairs.

"We'll be able to get jobs there soon. As tour guides." Flora hurried after him.

Despite objections, the quad bike was liberated once more. The frigate *Unicorn* awaited them.

Chapter 24

Signs pointed to the fact that there had been people down in the bilges. Not entirely surprising, given the ship was a tourist attraction. Tourists struggling right to the very end of the bilges would be a surprise, though. It was cram packed with building materials at the moment. Fergus and Flora had seen a couple of people come down, peer around and then scurry back up the stairs again.

There were no more messages, but the door had been opened. The hair was gone. The hieroglyphics had also been rubbed from the hull. They'd obviously done their job.

"I'm a hundred percent convinced that they're using the hidey-hole to store stolen objects," said Fergus. "And maybe even to pass notes."

"I'd bet Charlie on the fact you're right."

"So it looks like Ahmed's definitely involved in this."

"Let's tell the police." Flora's voice didn't match her words.

"No way, Jose. One, they won't believe us. Two, he'll know we're on to him."

"Three, we're doing it ourselves."

"That's the ticket."

"You don't half talk weird at times."

"So kill me."

"Don't say that. I might do it." She cackled for good effect.

"You say *I'm* weird."

All day they played with words, sitting in Fergus's room in front of a fan. Not their favourite occupation in the school holidays, but it paid off. Fergus suddenly jumped up and said, "I think I've got it," and did a dance of victory.

Flora joined him before flopping on to the floor, breathing heavily. Once she could speak she said, "Are you gonna enlighten me, Geekmeister?"

"Five lines. Take the five words on the first line. They're the first words of five new sentences. Look—"

> Charon
> Statue
> Justice
> Ship
> Leans

"The next five words are the second words of the sentence."

> Charon stalks
> Statue bull
> Justice always
> Ship holds
> Leans races

Flora grabbed the pen from him and tried it for herself. The completed missive:

> Charon stalks father of lies
> Statue bull secret place kept
> Justice always with righteous men
> Ship holds small key safe
> Leans races flying reign jumps

She threw the pen on the floor and said, "It's a bit more readable. Not much."

"I don't like the 'Charon stalks Father of Lies' bit."

"Isn't Charon the fella that whips the dead over to the other side?"

"He is. That means if Father of Lies means my dad, he's going to die." He grabbed his inhaler, shook it and uncapped it. Realising he didn't actually need it, he replaced the cap.

"Don't be so daft. He's in jail. Nothing could happen to him there."

"People die in jail all the time."

"And you say *I'm* a drama queen." Flora's stomach was churning. No way she was confirming her bestie's fears. Piling on his pain was not an option. "What about the rest of the riddle?"

Hands shaking, Fergus snatched up the paper.

"The next line's easy. It's saying where to pick up the next stolen object."

"Yep. The hidey-hole in the *Unicorn*. What's the next lot about?"

"I know what it means literally. D'you think it's got a hidden meaning?"

"Damned if I know."

"Mind your language, Miss Flora. My mum'll have a fit if she hears."

"Thought your parents were liberal."

"Not when it comes to swearing."

"Sorry. Someone sounds like they're in a giant huff about something."

"You know, you might be right."

"Adults have double standards. They tell us kids off for strops, but they're worse than us."

"Agreed. The next line is back to the ship and the hidey-hole."

That decided, they then stared at the last line as though a genie would appear to enlighten them. It didn't work.

After several minutes Fergus said, "They must be random words thrown in to make the riddle harder."

"Let's hope you're right. I've no better explanation."

Opening the Tomb

This was the stuff dreams were made of. An Egyptologist's dreams, that is. An undiscovered tomb, about to be entered for the first time, was rare indeed. Duncan Bernstein and Ahmed Minkah posed for photographs. They barely concealed their impatience. Money dictated they smile sweetly, so that is what they did. Then they turned to the tomb and walked through the door.

This was not a large tomb but it contained many treasures. The pair stood in wonder. Then the slow process of cataloguing and transporting the riches began. Gold beyond measure, jewellery, cups, bowls—all the trappings a Pharaoh would need for the afterlife. A sarcophagus so beautiful, it rivalled Tutankhamun's. Some minor mummies, presumably servants killed for no other reason than to serve the Pharaoh when he moved over to the other side. It wouldn't do for someone of his rank to be without servants. Time would tell who and what they were.

It was many months before the sarcophagus was opened. Slowly, gently, the lid was lifted off by four strong men. It contained a perfectly preserved mummy. And a dagger. Duncan indicated that Ahmed should be the one to pick it up. He was, after all, Egyptian. Ahmed held it aloft.

The curse was free once more.

Chapter 25

They heard a phone ringing. Fergus went to stand up but someone else answered it. His mum had obviously returned from her mysterious travels.

A few minutes later, Rad crashed through the door of his bedroom. "Your dad's been taken to Ninewells Hospital." The keys to her jeep were swinging from her hand. She was fairly smartly dressed in a suit and scoop top. A complete turnaround from her usual paint-streaked attire.

"What's wrong? I'm coming with you." He flew up, ready to follow.

His mum was already half way out of the door. "No. I'll call you when there's news."

"But ..." He was talking to her back.

"I really think we should tell the police about all of this," said Flora.

"What are the police going to do about a curse?" He paced back and forward, his body rigid.

"They might interview Ahmed."

"On the word of a couple of teenagers? I don't think so."

"We've got to do something."

That something included cooking dinner. Then throwing the dinner in the bin and cleaning the kitchen. Rad had enough on her plate without coming back to Armageddon.

The news, when Rad phoned, was devastating. Duncan was in intensive care in a coma.

"He's on a ventilator to help him breathe. Go home with Flora tonight. I'm staying here."

Chapter 26

What else could go wrong? They had to solve this, and solve it fast, before the curse claimed its next victim. This was coming far too close to home. They weren't out of their comfort zone; they were in orbit.

Despite Rad's protestations that they should stay home, they took the bus up to the hospital. It followed a circuitous route and took an hour and a half. They sat in gloomy silence the whole way, both lost in their own thoughts.

When they tipped up at the intensive care unit, Rad took one look at them and her fury erupted. This wasn't something they saw often in the usually affable Rad.

Fergus was sure her angry voice could be heard from intensive care to the main concourse. This was some feat, given the size of the hospital. He winced and stood up straighter, ready to face the full force of her anger.

"I told you to stay put. How dare you disobey me!"

Flora decided silence was best and left it to Fergus.

"I'm really sorry, Mum." Tears coursed down Fergus's face.

Rad remained unmoved. She'd lost weight since her husband had been locked up, and ropes of veins could be seen on her face. "Why are you here?"

"To see Dad and ask you some questions."

"You can't see him. No one is allowed in."

He took a deep breath, swallowed and said, "Does 'Father of Lies' mean anything to you?"

"Why are you asking about the devil? I've enough to be worrying about without you acting up."

"I seem to be hearing it a lot."

"Ask whoever is saying it."

He thought it would be better to move on. "Are things all right between Dad and Ahmed?"

"We haven't seen much of him recently."

"Even when he's in Dundee?"

"They've been busy. Your dad's been putting together a plan for another dig in Israel."

"Is Ahmed involved in that?"

"No. It's a Jewish dig. He can't get a visa."

"What does he think of that?"

"How do I know? For heaven's sake, Fergus. Stop asking stupid questions and go home."

"One more question. Did Ahmed visit Dad in jail?"

"I don't know. Why are you so obsessed with Ahmed? He's not involved in this. He's one of your dad's strongest supporters."

Fergus pulled at his hair and opened and closed his mouth a couple of times.

"Stop with the stranded fish impressions and answer me." Rad ran her hands through her long hair. The grey seemed a lot more evident to Fergus.

"I just wondered what he thought about the dagger and Dad's arrest."

It sounded a bit daft now that he'd said it out loud. He turned to go, grabbing Flora's hand and dragging her after him.

Before they left the hospital, Fergus bought a coffee and a cheese sandwich in the café, which he took back up to Rad.

Flora waited in reception. She suspected Fergus needed a hug from his mum. He wouldn't want her to see it. *By this point in the day my mum's probably too drunk to hug anyone.* She passed the time by ringing Bella to make sure she was all right.

91

Chapter 27

It was much too hot for sleeping. The next morning Fergus looked as though he wasn't far from intensive care himself. Flora offered him cereal, which he turned down. None of it was healthy enough for him. For someone who ate so much chocolate, he wasn't half funny about food, she thought. She managed to tempt him with whole-wheat toast and honey. He nibbled at it.

"What's the next step?" she asked. "Best to focus on the investigation."

"I've not heard from my mum."

"That's a good thing. Your dad must be hanging on in there."

He looked at her. There wasn't a glimmer of a smile in his eyes.

"Can I use your computer? I want to search the web. See if I can drag anything up about Ahmed."

"'Course. You take the main one. I'll use the laptop."

Bella wandered in. She stopped dead when she saw Fergus and her eyes widened. Then she hurtled over and gave him a tight hug. "What you doin' here?" She giggled. "In your jammies."

"My dad's not very well. My mum's up the hospital with him."

"Okay. My cousin's a nurse. She'll look after him." Bella's Down's meant that she had total confidence in every adult in her orbit. She also had a great deal of trust in the medical profession. Her Down's came with a heart condition for which she'd had several operations. She turned her attention to shaking cereal into a bowl.

Leaving her to it, Flora and Fergus went to the study and opened up the computers.

For an archaeologist involved in the most famous digs in recent years, there was very little to be found. Much of what they did find was buried behind newspaper paywalls. There was nothing for it but to pay a visit to the library archives. They'd get access there.

With the librarian's help, they were soon sifting through old newspaper articles. Some were digitised. Some were dusty paper copies that made them sneeze.

"Seriously, I feel like I'm at school, having to read the newspaper," said Flora. "What teen reads newspapers?"

"Moan. Moan. Moan. Have you actually read these articles?"

"No."

"Well, get on with it." He shoved her paper and pen closer to her.

After twenty minutes of in-depth reading of various articles, Fergus said, "This is bizarre."

"I'm not gonna argue."

They'd both picked up on the same strange point.

The headlines were all variations of:

'Scottish Archaeologist in Most Important Discovery
since Tutankhamun'
'British Man Discovers Most Important Egyptian
Tomb'
'Scottish Archaeologist, Duncan Bernstein, Given
MBE for Tomb Discovery'

The articles that lay under the headlines all went on to discuss at length the importance of Duncan's discovery. There was barely a mention of Ahmed.

"I didn't know your dad had an MBE."

"He doesn't talk about it," Fergus said with a shrug. "Not much there about Ahmed, is there?"

"They're British papers. Not likely to talk about anyone else."

"Good point."

With the librarian's assistance, they did an international search. Same result. Everything was about Duncan.

"Ahmed barely gets a mensh. Even in the Egyptian papers," said Fergus.

"If it was me, I'd be furious. He seems quite calm about it all."

"Is he though? Maybe he's carrying a white-hot grudge against my dad."

"If he did, it might explain the Father of Lies part."

"Whadda you mean 'might'? I think it does. He's calling my dad the devil. He must think he's a liar for taking all the credit."

"Why would he steal the dagger, though?"

"Don't know. It's Egyptian, so it'll be going back there anyway."

They gazed at each other, perplexed. Nothing they uncovered was making any sense.

Chapter 28

I want back in your dad's computers. If we look in all the files there might be something there."

As they were packing up, both of the Detective Duo's phones pinged. It was Tegan, saying that Stace's funeral was on the Friday at 10.00 am. The school was encouraging them all to go.

They barely had time to process this news when their phones pinged several times in quick succession. Friends were breaking the news that Daryl Chase had been in a serious accident while walking along the cliffs in Cornwall.

It looked as if the dagger had struck again.

Fergus was scrutinising his messages trying to take it all in. His phone rang.

"'S up, Mum." He listened. "On my way."

Flora raised a jaunty eyebrow.

"Dad's coming off the breathing machine thingy."

"That's a good thing, right?"

"Dunno. They've called me and all my brothers in."

"Is Lewis here from France?"

"Yeah. With Dani and the kids."

"You want company?"

"Better go on my own."

She pulled out her wallet, opened it, and handed him a twenty pound note. "Get a taxi. I'll sort all this out. You just go."

He dumped the books he was carrying on to the table. "Thanks. See you later."

At a loss for something to do, Flora strolled towards the *Unicorn*. They'd bought season tickets, so she thought she'd have another scout around.

"You again?"

The guide still hadn't forgiven her. Flora was thinking of gifting her a copy of the Bible—with the passages on forgiveness highlighted.

"I'm doing research."

"During the holidays?"

"I wanna be an archaeologist. I'm studying history." Flora arranged her features in an angelic manner. *I'm Oscar winning material.*

The woman's face looked less like a gargoyle and assumed a teddy bear appearance. "Where's your handsome pal?"

You're a bit old to be thinking of a fourteen-year-old boy that way. She squeezed out a few tears and a half sob. "He's at the hospital. His dad's dying."

The woman ushered her on board and gave her the freedom of the ship. "Call if you need us to help with anything."

Her acting skills were wasted. There was nothing to see. She attempted to open the door of the hidey-hole but no joy. She used the edge of a nail file, but the door remained resolute. It would not budge. *Weird. We've been able to open it every other time.*

In the absence of any other ideas, she decided to do covert surveillance. On the telly this involved sitting around in cars and watching a house. The lack of a car was a slight problem. She overcame it by sitting on a bench a little way down the quay and putting her headphones on. She would listen to music. No one would pay any notice to a teenager with headphones. It afforded her a superb view of the frigate. If anyone approached, she'd clock them immediately.

Chapter 29

He backed away from the bed until his back was against the wall of the private room. He felt the cool plaster and moved his hands over it. The family crowded round his dad's bed. The gathering was completed by a brace of burly coppers. Fergus stared at the shiny leather of their boots, incongruous in such a setting. Despite being in a coma, Duncan was handcuffed to the bed.

The shrill beep of a heart monitor pierced Fergus's every thought, making it hard for him to create any sense of order from the chaos.

"Come over here, Fergus." His mum's voice was weak. He could barely hear it even in the small room. Due to his father's status as a prisoner, they had him on his own away from other patients. Hovering policemen tended to get in the way in an intensive care unit.

Fergus couldn't move. Couldn't will himself to put one foot in front of the other. The smell of antiseptic, and something he couldn't identify, was overpowering. His stomach went into spasm and he thought he was going to throw up.

"He's not as bad as he was," said his mum. She looked worse than Duncan. Her eyes were lifeless, with dark rings under them that seemed to take up half her face. She was holding Duncan's hand. It was more clutching than holding given the limitations of the handcuffs. Her wrist was so thin it looked as if it would snap in a full north wind.

Fergus thought his dad must have looked ghastly before.

He was almost knocking on heaven's door now. He managed to force some words out. "Is he gonna die?"

"He's past the worst. Come and talk to him. He can hear you."

By sheer willpower Fergus managed to cross the chasm to the bed. He stared at his father.

The policeman put a gentle hand on his shoulder. "Not too close, son." Despite his size, his voice was soft.

Duncan started muttering. "No. No. Both. Not me. Please."

"What's he talking about?" asked Fergus

"It's just nonsense," replied his mother.

"Ahmed. Friend. Stop. Stop. No. Curse."

"Is he saying Ahmed's cursing him?"

"Don't be so daft, Fergus. The curse isn't real. You know that," said Lewis, his oldest brother.

"It was a publicity stunt," added Adair.

Murdoch, who'd hastened back from his church camp, wasn't saying much.

"You on drugs again?" asked Fergus. "Fine time if you are."

"No, I am not. Stop being such a brat." Murdoch stood up and took a step towards Fergus.

"Boys!"

They all swivelled towards the sound. It had come from their father.

He still had his eyes shut, but for the first time Fergus thought he might live.

Even the coppers looked more cheerful.

The family gathered round his bed, all chattering at once. Their mother stepped in. "Enough. Your dad needs rest, not you lot shouting in his lugs." She waved in the direction of the door.

They took the hint and drifted off.

Fergus hung back and said in a low voice, "It's going to be okay, Dad. This'll all get sorted."

Duncan opened his eyes and stared straight at Fergus. It seemed to Fergus that there was a hint of a smile in them.

His mum walked him to the concourse.

"Dad is gonna be okay, isn't he?"

"He'll recover. The doctors are confident there's no lasting damage."

Fergus blinked several times to clear away the tears that suddenly filled his eyes. He needed to be strong for his mum. She briefly put an arm round his shoulders. He glanced at her sideways. *Is this the right time to ask? Maybe 'cause Dad's getting better it might be.* He decided to risk it.

"Mum, can I ask something?"

Rad, pulled from her thoughts, looked startled. Her head turned and she peered at Fergus. "You know you always can, Fergus. Spit it out."

"Has there ever been any trouble between Dad and Ahmed?"

"No. Why do you keep asking?"

"Dad seemed to get a lot of attention when the dagger was found."

"Ahmed didn't mind."

They were approaching the front door so Fergus sped up his words. "Was that Dad's doing?"

"No. The world's press. They said he was like Howard Carter and Lord Carnarvon."

"Did Dad try to include Ahmed?"

"At first. Then he gave up."

Rad kissed him. For once he didn't object. She wandered back inside; he strode off in the direction of the buses. He pulled out his phone and sent a text to Flora. He'd meet her in town.

Chapter 30

Flora sat frying in the sun for twenty minutes. Not a single person had gone anywhere near the *Unicorn*—neither in nor out. *I don't think much of this surveillance lark. It's way more than just bein' boring. It's off the stratosphere boring.* She shifted on the bench so the sun wasn't beating down on the same spot. The Factor 50 cream she'd put on was struggling to keep up. Her mum might be a nut job, but she was obsessed with sunburn. Flora was banging her head along to 'Black Swans' by Leturgica when she noticed a likely prospect. A small ginger-haired man walked towards the frigate. His steps were fast and purposeful. In his hand was a small holdall.

She jumped from the seat and followed him. He disappeared down the staircase. Flora hesitated, wondering whether to follow him to the bilges. She came down on the side of caution. The bilges were small and given the lack of people on board that day she'd stand out like a sore thumb. If this was one of the gang of thieves and she scuttled along the bilges behind him, he'd work out in a flash what she was doing. Wild scenes of her being clunked on the head and thrown into the water played through her mind. In the end she scrutinised a display just inside the door. To be honest, she could have given a talk on its contents by now.

Ten minutes later he was back and hurrying off the ship. He was still carrying the bag.

Flora gave him time to disappear and then darted down to the bilges. Her pace slowed the lower she got, but she still slipped down the last step and sprawled on the deck. Her yellow T-shirt was filthy but she wasn't injured. She rubbed at the worst of the dirt and carried on. Carefully. The door to the hidey-hole was now open. There were a few scribbled hieroglyphs on the previously clean wall. Her phone was pressed into service once more. This time she took a video as well as photographs.

Flora's concentration was broken by a prickling in the back of her neck. She peered into the dim light, straining to detect anything out of the ordinary. She shuffled around to get a better view. She could see nothing. Was that a faint sound? She listened for a moment. All she could hear was the soft creaking of timbers, the sound of the wooden hull expanding in the heat. *Get a grip, Flora. You're jumping at shadows.* Nevertheless, she rattled through what she was doing and left the boat.

Chapter 31

They met up at McDonald's. Fergus had recovered his appetite and wolfed down a bean burger and large fries. Flora had difficulty keeping up with him.

"I take it your dad's improved."

"A bit. We think he told us off."

"Told you off? I've never heard your dad get mad."

"He doesn't often. I was fighting with Murdoch."

"Sensible move over a deathbed."

Fergus opened his mouth but she jumped in.

"Figure of speech. Sorry."

"The curse doesn't seem to have killed him off. It could carry him off to prison for a long time, though."

She brought him up to speed with what she'd seen at the *Unicorn* and showed him the photos of the hieroglyphs. There weren't many. Fergus got busy with the free WiFi and a new hieroglyphic app he'd found. Meant for schoolkids, it was a bit basic, but with his existing knowledge it did the trick just now. He soon had the message translated.

> Large Building stands proudly
> Sea pounds, roars beside
> 5 Windows Long

"Why can't they just leave normal messages?" asked Flora with a groan.

"To torment us?"

Flora punched him.

"They don't want just anyone reading them, dummy," said Fergus, rubbing his arm.

"Right back at you."

"The only large building by the sea round here is Broughty Ferry Castle."

"Why wouldn't they say castle?"

"No hieroglyph for it."

"Of course. Soz."

"To Broughty Castle." He screwed up his burger paper and lobbed it at the bin. It missed. He toyed with the idea of leaving it but his upbringing kicked in. He picked it up and deposited it safely.

"Via home. I need to get changed," said Flora.

"I'll get some transport and meet you there."

"The castle or my house?"

"The castle."

Chapter 32

Flora had changed from yellow to vermilion. The slogan on her T-shirt proclaimed: Free the Dundee one.

"What are you wearing?"

"It's a campaign to get your dad out of prison. I got you one as well. In black." She shoved a carrier bag at him.

"Seriously, what does it mean?"

"Do you live in a cave? Any campaign to get an innocent person out of prison uses this slogan."

"Never heard of it. It's a bit dramatic even for you. Where did you get them?"

"The Keiller Centre. Great, aren't they."

He just shook his head and wandered into the castle. Sometimes he wondered why they were friends.

The castle stood on a grassy knoll, flanked on one side by the beach and the other by the harbour. It was a beautiful sight, standing proudly against a Persian-blue sky. Built to withstand invaders in 1496, the castle had seen many a scene and battle. Today its biggest battle was the hordes of locals and tourists who were breaching its ramparts.

The Detective Duo could hardly move an inch. They moved around the outer courtyard at a snail's pace. They could barely see the cannons for kids crawling all over them like a horde of insects on a tasty treat. Their shrieks of delight joined the raucous screams of the numerous seagulls. Add in the chatter of adults and it formed a solid wall of sound that filled in any tiny chink between the bodies.

The number of people packed into the courtyard paled into insignificance compared to the crowds in the Tower House Museum. Apart from the cafés, this was one of the few places where a body could escape from the sun. The pair shuffled around the rooms looking for windows. There were none far enough down the walls to be reachable. As in most castles the windows were high and designed for protection rather than light.

"Looks like a dead loss," Flora shouted above the noise.

"I'm not giving up yet."

After another thirty more minutes of shuffling, even Fergus gave it up as a bad job.

"Let's try outside," he yelled.

Outside still had sun worshippers picnicking on the grass, but at least it was possible to weave between the bodies. They studied the castle walls. There were a number of windows. One row of circular holes was lower down. They took a closer look, but neither of them could reach anywhere near them. It seemed they were stymied.

"You could lift me on your shoulders," Flora suggested.

"I know you're wee but it sounds like a daft idea. One of us'll end up breaking something."

"So what's your bright idea, then?"

"The whole world'll be looking at us."

"Everyone's too worried about the heat and finding ice-cream cones. They'll just think we're a couple of kids mucking about."

Fergus thought for a moment, then gave in to the inevitable. He realised it was pointless arguing with Flora. She'd get her own way in the end anyway. He hefted her on his shoulders.

She looked in all the holes. Funnily enough, there was a small plastic packet inside one of them. There was also a seagull's nest. Mamma seagull was unhappy at the disturbance., which she proved by pecking at Flora's hand.

"Ow!" She pulled her hand back.

Fergus stumbled and tripped. They landed in a heap on the grass, Flora still clutching the plastic packet.

Closer inspection told them it was a ziplock bag with a sheet of paper inside. The deciphering of it would need to wait. There was an irate park keeper bearing down on them.

The parkie's tirade involved the words 'nuisance' and 'police'. They managed to convince him they were harmless, and he let them off with a warning. Visocchi's was calling out to them. Their ice cream had been cheering up residents and visitors for aeons.

Chapter 33

The café was equally packed. They managed to squeeze in at a tiny table right at the back. By good fortune it was also near a fan. Chocolate and vanilla ice creams ordered, they pulled the paper from the bag. They were expecting a code but were surprised. It mainly gave directions.

"Over to you, Geekmeister. I'm directionally challenged," said Flora.

"For someone so bright, you're not half stupid." He whipped out his phone and fired up the mapping software and spoke one word from the note: "Glamis."

"Glamis Castle?"

"Hope not. It would take us a decade to search. Cost a fortune as well."

"Anything smaller around Glamis?"

The phone did some further duty.

While he was searching, Flora took a large mouthful of her ice cream. Chocolate, caramel and vanilla—it was divine. The soft mixture danced on her taste buds and cooled her throat on the way down. It didn't get better than this.

Fergus followed her example. Once he had swallowed his banana and mango flavoured version, he said, "Angus Folk Museum."

"Never been. Is it big?"

"Not as big as Glamis Castle."

"Hidey-holes?"

"Tons. That will be our problem."

At the end was one sentence:

No fine resting place

Underneath that had been scrawled:

It is finished

"Sense that does not make," said Flora.
"I've brought the quad bike. Let's go."

Flora still wasn't sure about this mode of transport. It still terrify her, but she feared the pair of them could end up in serious shtook. Not only were they too young to be using the bike but they'd in effect nicked it as well. A police record did not bode well for either of their futures. However, despite her misgivings, she donned the protective clothing and hopped on. *You have to suffer at times to be a detective,* she thought. *Sherlock Holmes fell over a waterfall. Now that was suffering.*

Chapter 34

The man on the door took their money and left them to it. This gave them ample opportunity to rummage. Despite the holidays, the museum was surprisingly free of visitors.

"Didn't one of the other codes say something about a resting place?" Flora looked on her phone where she'd stored photos of everything.

Only those in the resting place know

"D'you think they're linked?" she asked.

"Could be."

They had a good look around. The only places to rest were the solid couches and the beds. The couches yielded nothing. Fergus lay on his back on the floor and looked underneath. Flora refused to get more clothes dirty. The beds it was then.

There were two wooden beds in wall recesses.

"They're quite cool," said Flora.

One was beautifully made up; both the bed recess and cover were elaborately decorated with exquisite lace. The other was less extravagant.

"Probably that was the one for the kids," said Flora.

"Pity help the poor sods who had to sleep surrounded by that frilly stuff. It would give me nightmares."

"Let's search the plain one. The note said, 'No fine resting place.'"

Flora shoved aside the sign that said, 'Fragile: Do Not

Touch.' A gentle search of the top of the bedcovers and the wood surround ensued. Nothing suspicious. Looking round to make sure they were still alone, Flora very slightly turned back the bedcover at the top. Nothing. She repeated this at the bottom. Concerned about fragility of the old fabric, she did it slowly and carefully. *I might be a detective, but I don't want to ruin our heritage.*

"Some poor soul slaved over making this and it's lasted for hundreds of years. I don't want to be the one responsible for knackering it."

"Delicately put."

"What are you? The language police? Who made you the boss of what I say?"

There was a dirty indentation in the mattress. She took some photos.

"Could we get some dirt for examination?"

"Get a grip, Flora. We're fourteen. How do you suggest we do that?"

"I was only sayin'."

It was a moot point as the doorman entered the room. "Stop touching the exhibits."

"Sorry. I'm doing research and wanted to see what it was like underneath."

That wasn't a lie, just a misrepresentation of the truth, she thought.

The doorman wasn't fooled. He showed them the way out.

"We're paying a lot of money to get heaved out the door," she said.

The doorman gave them their money back. Result.

"Looks like the antiquities are changing hands via tourist attractions," said Fergus on the walk back to the bike.

"It's a bit public, don't you think?"

"Not in that museum. Dead Dodos spring to mind."

"Do you think the dirty mark means something was hidden there?" Flora's voice held a hint of incredulity.

"In the absence of any other theory I'm sticking with that one."

Flora couldn't be bothered arguing. He was probably right. The Geekmeister usually was.

Chapter 35

"Much as I'm enjoying this, we've zero chance of solving it," said Fergus. "Not in time to save my dad."

"How's he doing? Any texts?"

"Not heard. Can't be any worse."

"Fancy inviting a few folks round tonight? We could have a movie night."

Fergus thought this was a jolly good idea. Even crime-solving detectives needed a night off now and again. Messages were sent to a few select people. Strict instructions were given not to pass it on. It didn't quite go to plan as they had twelve people rather than eight. One of the extras was Bella.

"You know I like movies, Fergus." She plonked herself down on the sofa with a huge bowl of popcorn.

It took some time for them all to agree on which movies to watch—and even then only after one person had stormed off. Finally they all settled down to the entertainment, and the investigation was put on the back burner for a few hours. The most they had to think about was a popcorn fight. Which Bella won. Her strategy had Fergus thinking they should recruit her as a detective. Bella might have Down's syndrome, but Fergus thought he'd rather like her on his side in any sort of battle. She was loyal and true, and fear didn't even enter her head. *Wish I could be more like you, my friend.*

Chapter 36

Fergus's mum came back early the next morning. She came through the door with a slight spring in her step and a hint of a smile on her face. She put her handbag down in the hallway and, after she'd made herself a herbal tea, took it into the sitting room. She stopped short, put her china cup down, and then marched to the bottom of the turret stairs.

"Fergus, get yourself down here now," she yelled.

No response, so she tried it in a louder voice and added, "If I have to come up those stairs you're in more trouble than you already are."

The thundering of footsteps sounded through the house and both Fergus and Flora appeared at the bottom of the stairs.

"What has been going on here?" There followed a ticking off that involved the words 'irresponsible', 'uncaring' and 'tidied'. The accompanying scowl and hand waving added gravitas and import to every single solid word.

This meant the pair spent the morning on cleaning duties. Flora was not absolved. In Scotland being a bestie meant you were part of the family. It also meant you were equally culpable of any wrongdoing. Result: any parent could dole out punishment and you had to comply. Flora had discovered this fact many years ago and had long accepted it.

"Sherlock Holmes and Watson didn't have to clean," said Flora.

"They didn't have mothers."

"Or popcorn."

Fergus's Uncle Gerunt turned up and gave them a hand, so it went more quickly, and they were freed from the shackles of slavery by lunchtime. He also slipped Fergus fifty pounds.

"Early birthday present. I'm sure you can use it during the summer."

"Thanks, Unc." This had cheered him right up. That and the fact his father was talking again.

"What have you been doing with yourself?"

"Nothing much. Too worried about Dad."

"I'm pretty worried myself. I'm sure it will all come out right in the end, though. Your dad's a good man."

On that cheery note Gerunt went off to find Rad.

"Blimey. Wish I had a relative who splashed the cash," said Flora.

"What shall we do with it?"

"Nothing. We've an investigation to run. The Hardy Boys didn't stop just because they got some money."

"They would only have had a couple of bucks."

"You'd argue with your shadow. What are we going to do next?" asked Flora.

"Visit my dad. We'll make him 'fess up."

"You're so tough. Least, I'd think you were if I didn't know you better. " She laughed and Fergus joined in.

Duncan had been moved from intensive care to high dependency. They were informed they could have a few minutes with him and that was it. He was propped up in bed, still attached to a plethora of machines, but had the faintest hint of colour in his cheeks, which relieved some of Fergus's anxiety.

"Hi, Dad."

"How on earth did you get in here?"

"A nice nurse said we could have a wee while. You're still not looking so good."

"I feel better than I look."

With the way his dad was looking, Fergus wasn't sure if he should carry on with his plan of asking numerous questions. At the end of an internal battle, bravery and desperation won over caution. He straightened and pulled back his shoulders.

Duncan wasn't in a fessing up mood. He didn't look like any mood other than grim.

"Leave this alone, son. You'll get hurt."

"What's going on between you and Ahmed?"

"Nothing."

"I thought you were pals."

"We are. This is nothing to do with you, Fergus."

"Are you still pals?"

"Fergus. You're like a locust. You never give up."

"Why won't you tell me?"

"Things have been a bit cool recently. He blames me for the dagger going missing."

"Did you steal it?"

"Of *course* not. Stay away from Ahmed. Do you hear me? Do not go near him under any circumstances."

Fergus hesitated. "Dad, are we broke?"

His father sat up slightly. Then quickly sank back. He drew in a sharp breath. "Whatever gave you that idea? Not in the slightest. Quite the opposite, in fact."

"In that case, can I have a new phone? I dropped mine in the water at Broughty Ferry."

"Speak to your mum. Tell her I said it's fine."

As the policemen were glaring at him, Fergus thought it was time to leave.

"Only you could go in to interrogate someone and come out with a new phone," said Flora admiringly as they exited the room.

"Good, innit." Fergus grinned broadly.

As they walked through the vast concourse, Natasha Cassidy, one of their classmates, came flying out of the café.

She was all wild-haired and red-eyed and wouldn't have been out of place in a horror movie.

"I want a word with you. All this curse stuff's your fault." The girl glared at Flora.

"My fault? Are you right in the head?" Flora attempted to shove past but Natasha pushed back.

"You're cursing everyone. Anyone you don't like ends up dead or injured."

"What are you talking about? I've no time for your ranting. Shove off, you stupid cow." The glint in Flora's eye said her short fuse was about to reach its end point.

"Have you seen the news?"

"Not for the past few hours. Some of us have a life."

Natasha pulled out her phone, opened up an app, and typed in "Dagger's Curse". Flora took the phone and Fergus peered over her shoulder. The internet was full of gloom and doom about the Curse. It was also blaming the curse for a teenager called Derek Gregory being knocked down by a car. He was in Ninewells Hospital in a critical condition.

Del was one of their school friends. He was also Natasha's boyfriend and had been at the museum with them. That was now three of their school friends affected.

"Call that curse back right now, Flora MacDonald."

"I can't control the curse."

"You're putting it on everyone," yelled Natasha.

"No, I'm flaming well not. You're insane." Flora's voice was equally loud.

Heads started to turn. Fergus stepped in to calm the situation down.

"Hush, Flora," he said urgently and tried to pull her away.

It had the opposite effect. Natasha turned on him.

"Your father started this. Why did he have to steal that dagger?"

"He didn't …"

Natasha's father dragged her away.

Flora, breathing heavily, stared after her. "Seriously? How can she believe that I can control that stupid curse?" Her eyes were wild and she had the look of someone who could punch the next person who came into her orbit.

Fergus just looked miserable. He put one foot in front of the other and trudged towards the entrance.

Flora followed, still clenching her fists. Deep in her heart she was wondering if Natasha was right. Were her thoughts somehow controlling the curse?

Chapter 37

They were fresh out of ideas so it was back to tailing Ahmed.

"We could tail the ginger-haired man I clocked," said Flora.

"How do you suggest we do that, genius? We don't know who he is."

"Well, I don't know. Why don't you think of something, genius, instead of dissing me?"

"Bickering isn't going to help us."

They got back into disguise. Flora was dulled down again. Fluorescent pink and orange did not lend itself to staying unnoticed. She vowed to buy a different outfit if they continued their detective career. They rang the changes with the sunhats, and different sunglasses were employed. They were good to go.

Ahmed was in the café bar of the Apex Hotel, with a friend, when they arrived. Fergus and Flora bought cold drinks and walked around the seating area, entering as far away from Ahmed as possible. They slipped amongst the tables and plonked themselves behind a humongous plant pot. It contained a magnificent fern. Together, these made the perfect barrier for listening incognito. The Duo sat in silence, their ears straining to hear.

"What can you bring me, my esteemed friend?" said Ahmed.

"I am honoured to be named thus." His companion had an Eastern European accent.

"Do they always waffle on like that?" muttered Flora. She used a Welsh accent just in case she could be heard.

"Shush. We'll miss something."

"Unlikely," she muttered, then shut up. *This patience lark is killing me. I was born for swashbuckling adventure, not all this hurry up and wait.* She dragged her thoughts back to the room, hoping she hadn't missed anything. Then she had a brainwave and switched her phone to recording mode.

Fergus looked at her, smiled, winked and nodded. His thumbs up signified *awesome idea.*

"I have a fine cow for sale," said Ahmed's companion.

"Is this cow pedigree?" asked Ahmed.

"It has a long history of being so. Many people seek it for its magnificence."

"Where may I see it?"

"It is currently at Cairnie Farm. You may view it there."

"Does it have companions?"

"No. The cow is lonely. It seeks suitable companions."

"Thank you, my friend. I will go immediately. I have been looking for a cow such as this."

"Should you wish it, we will agree an appropriate price."

"I am sure the price will be beneficial."

They shook hands and Ahmed stood up.

The detectives gave him a five-minute start and then bolted for the quad bike.

It was a long way to Cairnie Farm. The place was a working farm but also a tourist attraction. People came from far and wide to take their kids to the adventure park and pick fruit. Hence, nearly every child in Scotland had been there at some point in their life.

"The quad bike's not much of a match for a Mercedes," said Flora. "He'll be gone before we get there."

"Ah, but you forget, we can do it as the crow flies. He has to take every winding, tourist-packed road from here to the farm. We'll be doing it over fields once we get over the bridge to the Kingdom of Fife."

"Maybe you are a genius after all." Flora donned her gear, flung her leg over the bike, seated herself firmly and held on for dear life. Over hill and dale sounded somewhat bone-shaking to her. She'd rather like to get there and back in one piece.

Chapter 38

Fergus had the top of the range quad bike doing full speed ahead. Flora held on and prayed the whole way. As she had feared, it was a bone-juddering journey. By the end she wished she were already dead.

"Seriously, Fergus. How can you think that's fun?"

"It's awesome. The freedom."

"It's the inner circle of hell." She'd been reading Dante in Advanced English Club at school.

"C'mon, drama queen. We've an Arab to follow."

They used some of Gerunt's money to get in to the tourist attraction. Summer sun and fresh berries had the tourists out in droves.

"Sherlock got paid to do his investigations, you know," said Flora.

"I'll buy you some strawberries. Will that keep you happy?"

"Throw in a slice of cake and it's a deal."

They moseyed around the farm looking for likely places where they might see Ahmed. Not a sighting. They had a go on the trampolines with the idea that they wouldn't look too suspicious. In fact, they were more conspicuous, as the park bit was for kids. They enjoyed themselves anyway, and it was possible to see more of the park and farm as they jumped. Flora spotted him while she was mid bounce. They jumped off and rammed their shoes on.

"I've got a stone in mine," said Fergus as he was running.

"Suck it up," Flora said unsympathetically. "Sherlock—"

"Yeah. I know. Sherlock wouldn't have cared."

They followed Ahmed outside and saw him place a black canvas bag carefully in the boot of his car. He moved things around and then climbed in and drove off.

"A couple of quid says that's the missing cow statue."

"Yep. All one million five hundred thousand pounds of it."

"Stored in a field."

Fergus turned and headed towards the café.

Flora struggled to keep up with his long strides. "Hang on. Where are you going?"

"To buy strawberries."

"We need to follow Ahmed."

"On a quad bike? We'd be seen at a million paces."

They squandered some more of the money on cake, strawberries and milkshakes and took them to a table. There was silence while they consumed their feast. Fergus licked a piece of cream that was oozing from the side of his massive apple turnover. Flora was too busy eating her equally large raspberry and chocolate cheesecake to notice.

Once he'd finished, Fergus sat back in his chair, stretched his legs out and said, "They found a piece of cake that was over four thousand years old in a tomb."

"The ancients took cake to the afterlife? Respect."

"They spent a lot of time in the afterlife. You'd think they'd want more than one slice of cake."

"Maybe it was an ancient Egyptian picnic. For the journey over the Styx." Flora picked up her napkin, spat on it and wiped chocolate from around her mouth.

"Bit better than a two-day-old brownie."

Fortified, they headed back to the bike and pointed it in the direction of Dundee. The return pace would have suited their grandmothers. Fergus wasn't sure his stomach would hold up against any bone jarring. They took the roads.

The Dagger's Journey

For hundreds of years the curse had lain dormant.

During this time, it did nothing but wait. Wait for the time it would be needed to protect its master once more. While the Pharaoh lay buried in his ornate tomb, he was safe. No need for constant vigilance.

As the first chink of light entered the tomb, the curse awakened. Its master, the Pharaoh, needed protection once more.

The mummy and the dagger were separated for the journey to Cairo. During the journey several accidents occurred, some leading to death. Sickness accompanied the convoy. Stories of the curse spread. Labourers downed tools and walked off the job. Museum employees refused to handle the shipment when it arrived. They were sacked and no one applied for the available jobs.

This curse did not confine itself to the lower classes. The senior curator of the exhibition at the Cairo Museum was murdered. A single stab wound to the heart. His body was found outside the museum in the early hours of a Tuesday morning by a cleaner. The police found the weapon, a dagger, still in place.

His replacement chose to display the mummy and the dagger together in a single sealed case. This was done for reasons of beauty rather than in response to the unfortunate circumstances. Whatever the reason, it appeased the curse. It waited once more.

Chapter 39

It was time to go to the police. Flora thought they had gathered too much information and things could get dangerous. Fergus agreed. This was getting way beyond their capabilities.

"I'm not sure they're gonna take us seriously, though," said Fergus.

"They've got to. We've shedloads of evidence. They can't ignore us."

"This is the police we're talking about and we're just a couple of kids."

Despite their misgivings, they each took a deep breath and climbed the stairs of the police station. They shoved open the door and found themselves facing a desk sergeant. It was the mountain they'd met previously.

"You two again? Your dad's not here anymore. He's serving at her Majesty's pleasure in Perth Prison or he's in Ninewells Hospital. Take your pick."

"We're not here to see Dad. We've got some evidence that might help him."

"I don't think so. What evidence could you come up with that the police haven't?"

"We have, Sergeant. Honest." Flora's lip was trembling again. This time she wasn't acting. She was terrified they'd both end up in bother. Her mother would ground her for life and fit a lock to her bedroom door.

The mountain melted yet again and went to talk to his superior.

They were ushered into a larger office than the previous one. This one had a window with a view of the car park. They told the senior officer everything they knew. He was both dismissive and furious.

"You are interfering with an ongoing investigation. This is a criminal offence."

"We're passing on what we know," said Fergus.

"You don't know anything."

"We know Ahmed Minkah is dealing in stolen antiquities," said Flora.

"You know no such thing. Mr Minkah has been fully cooperative."

Flora wasn't giving up without a fight. "That doesn't mean he didn't do it."

"Not only are you lying, you are committing slander. You might want to rethink your next statement, young lady."

"Is this all the thanks we get for helping the police?" demanded Fergus. "My dad's in jail for something he didn't do."

"So that's what this is all about. Leave the detecting to the police and run off and play."

The sergeant showed them to the door. He helped them through it with a little push.

"Miserable old goat," Flora muttered as she stomped down the stairs.

"Which one?" asked Fergus, with a wry grin.

"Both! But especially the sergeant. He just assaulted us. Police brutality is what it is."

"There's no way we're giving up the investigation now. That lot'll throw my dad in jail forever."

"Fighting talk. Are you gonna wear that T-shirt now?"

"I might just do that. 'Free the Dundee one' it is. We'll get my dad outta that jail."

Chapter 40

"Sod the lot of them. How dare they treat us like babies." Fergus was still mad three hours later.

"Calm doon, son. You'll have an asthma attack."

"I've never felt less asthmatic in my life."

"I'll ferret around in your dad's computer. Maybe there's something in there."

"Ferret away. We've already broken a million laws. Might as well carry on."

Flora opened up file after file. She searched for 'Ahmed' but very little came up. A few references to him being at the dig. He seemed to do very little digging and a lot of cataloguing. Not what she would expect from an archaeologist. They were usually foaming at the mouth to get their hands dirty.

She tried his surname. Nothing more.

She beat a tattoo of 'Scotland the Brave' on the desk. It helped her think. Something was tugging at her memory.

"Fergus," she yelled. "Bring our notes in. I need to check something."

He obliged and she riffled through them.

"Eureka. The cartouche says 'Father of Freedom', or something like that."

She searched the computer for the phrase. She got ten hits.

"Any chance of a cold drink?"

"What am I, a servant?"

"As good as."

He opened the fridge, pulled out a Coke and handed it to Flora. She popped the tab and slugged down the cooling liquid. "Aaahh. That hit the spot. I might have a bit more energy for the search now."

A rapid double click and one of Duncan's files was opened. It was some sort of journal. Flora skimmed it. Most of it made no sense until she came to a paragraph about Father of Freedom.

> The father of freedom watched us closely today. His face was inscrutable. He reminds me of the Sphynx. What was this Egyptian thinking as an international team of archaeologists unearthed his country's treasures. He does not say much but seems friendly. He assists us with the dig, but mainly catalogues everything.

She opened up another file.

> The Father of Freedom now works much more closely with us. His knowledge of Egyptian antiquities is unsurpassed. Without him our work would be much more difficult.

And another

> The Father of Freedom slipped away from camp today. Missing for five hours. He returned with no explanation.

"If Ahmed is the Father of Freedom then your dad always had his suspicions about him."

"They seemed to get on okay. I never noticed anything when I met him before."

"You were a kid. Kids never notice anything."

"True. I was too busy doing a small dig with Walid. That mainly meant getting dirty."

"They let a couple of kids on a dig?"

"I think they planted some bits that didn't matter. They treated us like kings when we found something."

"You're so lucky. Must have been awesome to grow up around digs."

"Totally."

"Back to the investigation. This is another strike against Ahmed."

"But my dad seemed to rate him at the same time. He never let any of us know he felt like this."

"It's curious. But the facts speak. Ahmed is our man." Flora lifted her hair from her neck and turned towards the fan. "I've never known it to be this hot."

"All we need to do now is catch Ahmed." Fergus seemed as cool as ever. The lad never seemed to break a sweat.

"Oh, is that all? We'll do it before teatime." She closed down the computer.

"We'd be hard pushed, seein' as it's teatime now."

If Flora had a choice of eating her tea or investigating, food won hands down. Fergus had other ideas.

"I think we should stake out the hotel and see if Ahmed goes anywhere in the night."

"Are you for real? No way! Even *my* parents might notice I was missing."

"Sherlock Holmes and Watson went out at night."

"Get it into your thick skull. They didn't have parents. Watson's wife might have given him some leeway. My mum won't."

"The original Flora MacDonald fled in the night with Bonnie Prince Charlie. *She* didn't worry about her mum."

"And she had Hanoverians after her and the Bonnie Prince." Flora thought about this. "Sod it, let's do it."

"Now you can have your tea."

While they were waiting for the food to heat, they discussed their strategy for the stake-out.

"Where's best to wait? I can't for the life of me picture the area."

Fergus thought for a minute. "I think there's a bench nearby. It is a bit sparse, though. There's a couple of huge potted palms at the entrance."

"No way I'm hiding behind a pot plant all night. You're unhinged."

"Okay. Strike the palm trees. We'll do a recce when we get there." Fergus, as always, knew it was better to work around Flora.

"We need a story in case the police come sniffing round. How about we're researching what it's like to be homeless."

"Good plan. Sherlock Holmes would love it. If they ask about our parents, we'll swear up the Sidlaws and down the Ferry that our parents know."

"You mean lie? Fergus, how could you?" She unwrapped a sweet and shoved it in her mouth. She then lobbed the crumpled paper in his general direction.

Fergus just grinned and Flora joined in.

"Now that's settled, where's my tea?"

She wolfed the food down the minute it was in front of her and dashed off to make an appearance at home. She could check on Bella, find something darker to wear, and escape from her room later.

Chapter 41

It was quite nippy later, so Flora stole into her sister's room to borrow a dark coloured hoodie. It would be bit tight, but it would just about do. She had hoped to get away with simply purloining it, but Bella was in there, playing on her computer.

"I'm just borrowing your hoodie," she said quietly, rummaging in the drawer to find it.

"You should wear your own clothes, Flora."

"I know, chickadee, but mine are all in the wash or at Fergus's house. You don't want me to get cold."

"Okay. You can borrow mine." Bella turned back to her game.

Flora was eternally grateful for her easy-going sister. Downs Syndrome didn't stop her doing what she wanted. She'd go far in life. Flora was going to make sure she supported her every step of the way.

By ten o'clock Bella was tucked up in bed. Flora went in to see she was okay. She was fast asleep and had kicked the sheet off. Flora pulled it halfway over her sister and then bent down to kiss her head.

She had a quick look in the sitting room. Her mum was comatose on the couch, early even for her. Her father was in his study. Walking across the hallway, she thought she heard the study door open. She froze. It was a false alarm brought on by her own overactive imagination. She slipped out through the front door without anyone noticing, took her bike and wheeled it out on to the quiet street. She threw her leg over the frame and kicked off, heading at full speed towards the main road. Well, as full speed as Flora could do. It would take her about half an hour to get to the Apex Hotel.

Fergus also made the journey by bicycle. The quad bike was speedy, but it made enough noise to waken a whole host of dead mummies. So pushbike it was. He took a couple of puffs of his inhaler and waited until it took effect. Then he kicked off and his bare legs got pumping at full speed.

They did a recce and spotted a bench just up from the front entrance. It was in the shadows and no streetlight illuminated it. Saying that, it was still fairly light. Scotland had oodles of daylight in the summer.

The stake-out was a needless exercise, as not a soul came by. Fergus had brought a couple of flasks of hot chocolate and a couple of bags of sweets. That kept them warm and gave them something to do. They each took turns to get some shuteye.

Morning came and there wasn't a sign of Ahmed. The days were ticking by, slowly sealing Duncan's fate. The dagger was also still missing. Something had to happen soon!

Chapter 42

At ten past midnight on the third night of the stake-out, Ahmed left the hotel. He strode over to his car and got in. The engine revved and he pulled off.

It was then that the stupidity of their idea hit Flora.

"How are we meant to follow a Mercedes on a bike? He'll be doing about a million miles an hour at this time of night."

Fergus grinned. "I put a tracking device on his car."

"O—M—G! I'm in awe. Where? How?"

"Pinched it from my dad's study."

"Why has he got them? He's not exactly Interpol."

"They put them on any vehicles transporting antiquities. If they're hijacked, they can track them."

"That's genius. So we can take our time."

"We can't go too slow. We need to catch him at something."

Pulling a reflector strip from her jacket, she said, "What are we waiting for?"

"Me to open the app up so we know where we're going."

That done, they set off. They were both hoping he wasn't going to Inverness.

After what seemed like hours, but was probably only forty minutes, the tracking app showed the vehicle had stopped. They were still about half an hour away if they pushed themselves hard. Fergus pedalled faster. With a maniacal look in her eye, Flora stood up and used the full force of her body to drive the pedals harder.

The destination was a small castle.

Chapter 43

A s they drew nearer, they ripped off the reflective strips and dimmed their lights. They hid their bikes at the entrance. Creeping up the driveway, they made sure to keep in the shadow of the trees.

Ahmed pulled away just as they got there.

"You have got to be kidding me. All this way and he's leaving," said Flora.

"Never mind that. Did he see us?"

"Dunno. Don't suppose so. It's pretty dark."

"He had his full beams on."

"If he'd seen us, do you think we'd be standing here chatting about it?"

"Good point. We'd probably be tied up and flung in his boot."

The flashlights on their phones were employed to scope the place out. Much of it was derelict. Vines and tree branches provided a vivid green blanket for the stones. Through the years, many had crashed to their final resting place on the ground. They were a trap for the ankles of the unwary.

One turret still stood like a watchman in the night. They were squinting to try and see it when an owl swooped low over their head. Flora choked back a scream. She backed into a tangle of branches and tumbled.

"Shush. If there's anyone here you'll waken them," whispered Fergus.

"Thanks for your sympathy." She kept her tone low.

"Are you okay?"

"Fine." She shone the flashlight over herself. "My jeans are torn and I've scraped my hand. 'Part from that it's all good."

A solid door, secured with a substantial padlock, blocked the entrance to the turret. Given this was the only entrance to the tower, they decided they were safe. They sat down, leaned against a wall and waited for some light. Preserving their phone batteries was a must. They'd never find their way home otherwise.

Somehow they both managed to doze off, forgetting that they should have maintained a watch. Fortune favoured them. It was the dawn chorus that woke them and not someone involved with the dagger.

They had a dribble of water left between them.

"I could eat a mouldy sarnie," said Flora.

"I'm so hungry I'd join you even if it was meat."

"I'm sure I heard a stream. Let's investigate."

In the morning light the castle looked even more crumbly, although the turret looked solid enough. Tangled undergrowth snatched at their ankles and progress was slow, but finally they came across a small stream. Debating whether it was safe to drink from, they threw caution to the wind. The water was cool and ran down their arms as they filled their empty drinks bottles. They gulped it down as though their lives depended on it. There were some wild raspberries just over the perimeter wall. Manna from heaven, or nectar from the gods? Neither cared. They pulled them from the branches and stuffed them in their mouths. Hands and faces were easily washed in the stream and dried on T-shirts.

"I feel frightfully Famous Five," said Fergus.

"We're a bit useless compared to them. They had supplies and lashings of ginger beer."

As the sun rose, it bathed the rocks, showing every one of their glorious colours. Insects scuttled from under them and hurried about their day. A bee buzzed past Fergus's ear and settled on a flower.

It was time to have a proper look around now that there was light aplenty. The place was locked up tight as a duck's backside. They rattled the padlock and tried to open it with a penknife, but it seemed as if it was titanium plated.

"You allowed to carry that thing around? Isn't it against loads of laws in Scotland? You'll be joining your dad in the nick."

"This tiddly little thing? I don't think so. It's got bits and pieces I use on digs."

It was difficult to believe that such a place could harbour evil. The shiny new padlock could indicate that something untoward was going on in the turret; it could also indicate the owner didn't want people traipsing around his property.

"D'you think the artefacts are being stored in here?" said Flora.

"Could be. Either that or they're using it as a dropping off point. Maybe the cow's in there."

"I feel like kicking the door down, but all I'd achieve is a broken foot." He did have a go at it and then hopped around clutching his toes. He could still walk, though, and the only thing hurt was his pride.

"Watch it, macho man. You need to ride home."

They searched some more and Fergus did find something. It was so well hidden it was a wonder he saw it.

"There's something in a crack up there." He pointed above his head.

Flora strained her neck to look up. "Are you sure?"

"The moss on either side's been disturbed. Someone or something has been up there."

Stretching to his full range, Fergus reached up. The object teased him by remaining just out of reach.

The pair heaved a large rock over. Beetles and ants scurried out from the darkness of their home. They slithered under neighbouring rocks. Steadied by Flora, Fergus stood on the rock and could just reach. He had the paper in his fingers.

"What a palaver," said Flora. "You'd think in this day and age they could just text each other."

"Wouldn't have been much use to us, though. They probably don't want to leave a digital footprint. The police would be on it like a wolf on a carcass."

"Ooh, listen to you being all knowledgeable about tech stuff. Fair point though."

They opened the note.

> All is gone
> To its roots it will return
> The curse contained
> Evil reigns within

"I need sleep to deal with this."
Fergus, for once, agreed.

Shipping the Curse

The dagger was removed from its case. Gloved hands wrapped it in soft cloths and placed it in a velvet-lined box. This was packed in a crate alongside twenty-three other principal artefacts from the exhibit.

The consignment was checked, double-checked and triple checked. At any point the dagger could have been removed and placed back in its case. It was not too late.

A sturdy lid was positioned on the crate. The sound of an electric screwdriver could be heard.

An address label was slapped on and the precious cargo began its journey to Scotland.

The curse accompanied it.

Chapter 44

It was a long, hot slog back to Dundee. Flora hadn't done so much exercise in years. She fell into bed without taking off her clothes. Seconds later she was dreaming of curses and ancient mummies. Even that didn't make her stir.

The ringing of her mobile phone woke her at one o'clock. Her hand swept over it and knocked it to the floor. She hung over the edge of the bed and grabbed it.

"Fergus, wad'ya want?"

"It's time to get up."

"I've had about three minutes sleep in the past four days. Go away." She pressed end call.

Forty seconds later it rang again.

"Wrack off."

"My dad's out the hospital."

She sat up and rubbed her eyes. They felt as though the contents of Bella's sandpit had been poured under the lids. "Is he home?"

"Get with the programme. Of course he's not home. He's actually on his way to Perth Prison."

"What! Why? Has the trial happened already?"

"Nope, he's been charged and he's there until his trial."

"I can't believe they're not looking for someone else."

"Why would they? They've got my dad."

"I'm coming over."

She swung her legs over the bed and put her feet to the floor. Pain shot right up her body and erupted through her head.

"What the …"

Bella came running in. "You okay, Flora?"

"Fine. Cycled too far yesterday. Seized up." Even her mouth hurt.

"You're a silly girl. My teacher makes us stretch before we exercise."

"She's a wise woman. I'll remember that in future."

She staggered to the shower. It was a fancy modern effort that had a seat incorporated in it. She lowered herself onto it. Powerful jets of water battered her body from several nozzles arranged around her. Steam filled the bathroom as the scalding water soothed her muscles.

Stoking up her martyr complex, she forced herself back on the bike. Her progress was unsteady but she managed the trip to Fergus's house. Mainly because it was downhill. She texted him and told him to come downstairs. Just the *thought* of climbing the stairs made her pain worse.

Fergus bounded down the stairs to meet her.

"How can you not be in pain after that ride?"

"I told you you were a knacker."

She vowed to herself she would go to the gym when all this was over.

"Now that you're here, we need a plan of action."

"We need lunch. I haven't had anything since those berries."

He gave her a huge piece of spicy frittata and some chocolate. She felt it was a perfectly balanced meal. Especially since she washed it down with a can of diet Sprite.

Fortified and reenergised, she was ready to decipher the latest clue.

"'All is gone'. Could mean the castle's empty," said Fergus.

"Could also mean they've nicked everything worth nicking."

"Maybe."

"The next line's saying that the dagger is going back to Egypt."

Fergus gave her that one. It was the most likely explanation. "The next two lines might be saying the dagger is inside the castle."

"You think?"

"We need to go back and stake the place out."

"There's absolutely no way I'm cycling back there."

"Quad bike it is then."

Chapter 45

They took the back roads and several times went off road. Flora grasped the lifeline that was the handlebars. Still she bounced around. She squeezed her knees hard against the frame. A couple of times her bottom lifted into the air. In a remote field, Fergus stopped the bike. There was nothing for miles. Apart from trees, that is. You couldn't go far in Scotland without finding a swathe of trees. They were like a legion of centurions guarding the land from invaders.

"Why are we here?"

"You're going to learn to drive this quad bike. You'll be less fearful."

"Not on your Nellie. What makes you think that's a good idea?"

"It's what Murdoch did with me."

"You're mad. Seriously unhinged. I know I—"

"Stop gnashing your teeth and get on the front."

"No. No way."

"We're not moving until you do. D'ya want to stay here all day?"

Flora sat down on the ground and a standoff began. Fergus pootled around taking photos of the view. In the next field he spotted a ewe with twin lambs and slipped close enough to be able to get a decent photo. By this time Flora realised he was serious about not going any further until she learned to control the bike. She gave in. They needed to get to the castle and this was taking up precious investigating time.

"Get on with it then," she shouted over to Fergus.

He talked her through everything while she carried out the actions. He rode the back of the bike, letting her do a short journey. He took her over uneven terrain and into the trees. A branch slapped her in the face. It gave her a shock, but the helmet protected her from injury. The same couldn't be said for her hands, which bore deep scratches. The whole thing took no more than five minutes but had her shaking.

She refused to go over ten miles an hour despite his exhortations to "give it laldy".

She'd be giving *him* "laldy" if she had her way. He was going to be so dead when they got back to Dundee.

Not a bright thing to think when there was a curse in the air.

Chapter 46

The castle was still locked up tight as an otter's derrière. Fergus hefted Flora onto his shoulders. She still couldn't reach the window to see in. A scout round the whole building resulted in cuts to their legs and nettle stings. Around the back there was a small hatch, hidden by tall undergrowth. It also had a rugged padlock swinging from the hasp. This was a padlock with superpowers. Someone meant business.

"Not used much, so why the new padlock?" said Flora.

"To keep prying eyes away."

"You don't say. It was a rhetorical question."

"You been reading the Oxford dictionary again?"

"If *you* read it, you might use a few different words. Same old tripe from you."

"Oooh. Cutting." Fergus's grin took the sting from his words. "Looks like some of the grass and weeds are broken. New ones growing through. I'd say the padlock's been there about four weeks."

"The Geekmeister strikes again."

"Ain't you glad?"

"Couldn't we drive the quad bike up here and use that to look through the window?" said Flora.

"Still not high enough. Besides, we'd give away that someone's been here."

"It's a castle. About a million visitors could have been here."

"You ever heard of it?"

She looked at him, her eyes narrowed.

"No, thought not. A tourist attraction this is not."

"What's your brilliant suggestion, then? You bein' an international spy and all."

"See if there's a way into the hatch."

Flora raised a cynical eyebrow and her face assumed a 'yeah, right' look. She followed him without saying a word.

They rattled and yanked at the hatch but it was going nowhere. The granddaddy of all padlocks held firm. The hatch fitted snugly so there was no way they were opening it from the side. Even if they had a crowbar. Which they didn't. They had nothing more than four bottles of lukewarm water and a couple of sandwiches. Not the best equipment for jimmying open a hatch.

"If we were Sherlock and Watson, we'd pick the lock."

"If we were Batman and Robin, we'd blow it open. Neither's going to happen."

"Use a stone to bash it open?"

Despite Fergus's scepticism, he gave it a go. The rock bounced off the wood and hurtled back. It missed Flora's foot by a micrometre. The door remained undefeated, with only a small scrape to mar its beauty.

"Got any cannonballs handy?" asked Fergus.

"Fresh out of them."

They walked the mile back to the quad bike to see if there was anything in the panniers that would help. Murdoch kept all sorts in the panniers, but they couldn't find anything that would meet their need. There was nothing for it but to return to Dundee in search of a sharp implement.

Chapter 47

Things didn't go quite as planned. When they returned to the house of the round turret, Ahmed was lounging in an armchair chatting to Rad. They tried to dash past the sitting room, but it didn't wash with Rad.

"Come in here."

Flora made an attempt to sidle off.

"You too, Flora."

Ahmed assumed an aggressive posture. If the eyes were a window to the soul, then Ahmed's soul was hell.

The pair dawdled, which brought them a sharp, "Get in here now."

Rad waited until they had fully entered the room before demanding, "What are you two up to?" Fergus opened his mouth to speak but she interrupted: "And don't say 'nothing'."

In the absence of anything better to say they kept silent. Flora shuffled her feet and stared around the room. Fergus feigned great interest in a scuff mark on the parquet floor.

"Ahmed would like a word with you."

The man stood up. He looked down at them through hooded eyes.

"Why have you been following me?"

Silence. More foot shuffling with added fidgeting.

"Answer the question," said Rad.

Flora decided on bravado. "We were following you. We thought we would learn something from such a highly esteemed gentleman." She was proud at the formality of her language. Not bad for a fourteen-year-old, she thought.

"You are children. You should not be poking around in my business. There will be consequences."

"There certainly will," added Rad. "Starting now. You will both apologise to Ahmed. Fergus, you are grounded for a week."

"No way. It's the holidays."

"You should have thought about that before you started meddling."

She turned to Flora. "Go straight home, young lady. I am ringing your mother."

Once they had apologised, Ahmed was his usual polite and formal self.

"I see no reason for such a punishment. Keep them in today, maybe. Then let them enjoy the sunshine."

Their thanks were more heartfelt than their apologies. One day was bad. A week would have been a catastrophe.

"I'll FaceTime you," said Flora on her way out of the door.

"No you won't. The grounding's virtual as well as real world." Rad's voice had a no-nonsense edge to it.

Flora stomped off, gritting her teeth. Shouting at Rad would only result in a week's grounding. Adults were so mean.

The Curse Unleashed

When the packing case arrived in the MacManus Galleries in Dundee, it had been travelling for two days. It was placed in a sealed vault over the weekend.

Monday morning brought a heatwave to the city. Two curators, assigned to oversee the Egyptian exhibition, opened the case and exposed the treasures within. It was two hours before the dagger was unwrapped. They admired the magnificent object.

The curse slipped out unseen.

By the afternoon one of the curators had been admitted to Ninewells with heat exhaustion. The curse had a grip on the city.

Chapter 48

The next few days brought news of more accidents and death. The curse was busy. Television, newspapers and social media were full of it. A young boy, son of one of the curators, was seriously ill in hospital. It was doubtful whether he would live.

Stonework had fallen off one of the older buildings in the city centre and several people were injured. Talk of the curse reached a crescendo and did not seem likely to die down any time soon.

Fergus and Flora knew none of this until they were allowed back into civilised society. Flora's mother had gone nuts at her and said she was grounded for two days. No amount of pleading would shift her. All electronic equipment was confiscated. This included her computer.

"It's the holidays. You don't need it," said her mum.

Given that Fergus was also incommunicado, Flora had to grin and bear it.

When they were released from their incarceration and their electronic devices were returned, the first thing they did was check for activity on their various accounts.

Tegan Gloag had texted Flora to say she'd broken her arm.

"During the holidays!!! Stupid Curse."

Flora texted back, leading to a text frenzy. The general gist was that Tegan was bored because of her broken arm.

"Do you wanna be our eyes and ears?" asked Flora.

"You got it. Any gossip, I'll pass it on."

Fergus checked his social media accounts for all things curse. It wasn't looking good out in the wide world. Snatching up his iPad, he FaceTimed his bestie.

"Have you seen the news?"

"Hello to you too. Yeah. Good and bad."

"There isn't any good. My dad's going to trial in three weeks."

"Oh! *Not* good."

"Not good at all. Mum says he could get twelve years."

"Not once we solve the case."

"Can't see that happening. We're banned and stalled."

"Ignore the ban and come up with something to unstall us."

They agreed to meet in Iced Gems in Broughty Ferry. They would need a slice of homemade cake to get them through the day. Sugar also helped the thought process.

Chapter 49

"Police Scotland have got a cheek," said Fergus. "'Call with information.' We *gave* them information. They chucked us, and it, out."

"Fascists."

"That's a bit steep. I was more going with idiots."

"Whatever. Useless lot."

Fergus opened a drawing app on his iPad and sketched out a map with the locations of all the stolen antiquities. He had inherited Rad's artistic skills. The map could have been used in any good treasure story. They all lay within a fifty-mile radius of Dundee. The castle was positioned somewhere in the middle, slightly nearer to Dundee.

"Do you think we should visit the museums?" asked Flora. The question in her voice was weak.

"Are you daft? It would take us all week. We've already lost a couple of days."

He bent over the map, then opened up another app on his iPad.

"What are you doing?" Flora took a humongous bite of her raspberry and white chocolate cup cake. She choked and spluttered cake all over Fergus's iPad.

"Oi. Watch it." He grabbed a napkin and wiped off the cake crumbs, then returned to his task.

Flora, having recovered the ability to breathe and talk, said, "Geekmeister, what ya doin'?"

"Will you shut up for a minute?"

She threw him a look that could freeze the River Tay and

pulled out her phone. No updates from Tegan. The rest of the skinny on social media was inane. No mention of the curse or any more disasters befalling the good citizens of Dundee. She opened up an archaeology app and started reading.

Ten minutes later Fergus said, "Got it."

"Oh, we're talking now?"

"Do you want me to tell you?"

"Hit me."

"I've triangulated all the places on the map. Plotted the centre of them all."

"This is important why?"

"I searched for any other abandoned buildings nearby. There's a broken down farmhouse. According to Google Streetview, that is."

"My favourite geek strikes again. Go Fergus."

The farmhouse was calling their names. The quad bike was once more pressed into service. Yet again they filled it with petrol. This was turning out to be an expensive investigation. It was draining their money and their time.

Chapter 50

It was late evening before they got there. Back roads and bumps don't lend themselves to speed. Fergus circled round the farm and parked behind a copse way back from the perimeter. Flora unscrewed the top from a bottle of Coke. A fountain of liquid erupted all over her purple shirt.

"Great. I'll attract every wasp and midgie from ten miles around."

"Yep."

Fergus was far too cheerful about it for Flora's liking.

"What do we do now?" she asked through clenched teeth, as she brushed ineffectually at her shirt.

"Drink up. Then we explore. If anyone's there, we'll say you were looking for a place to clean your shirt."

"If Ahmed's there, me and my shirt will be buried in the garden."

"Prob'ly. Or you'll talk your way out of it."

Despite Fergus's bravado, their pace was slow as they walked through the trees. A crashing sound made them jump. They stopped, their eyes wide. A small doe appeared. It was difficult to tell who was the most surprised. Fergus had the presence of mind to snap a photo on his phone. It wasn't often you were nose to nose with a deer. The doe changed direction and bounded off. They continued, hearts drumming in their chests. A movement caught Fergus's eye. He signalled Flora to stop. This time it was a red squirrel.

"I feel like I'm on a nature walk," said Flora.

"If we meet anyone, that's exactly what we're doing."

"Being an investigator is weird. Do you think Sherlock Holmes banged into deer?"

"If he ever went to Greenwich. There were deer in the park then."

"How do you know all this stuff? I mean, it's helpful, but seriously freaky."

"I read a lot. You should try it."

Finally they reached the farmhouse, which looked rather like a discarded kid's toy. Once a masterpiece, it was now a mess of bricks. They trod carefully over broken glass from the dangling window frames. One shuddered as they passed. Fergus yanked Flora a few steps away.

"If that comes down, it's taking your foot off," he whispered.

Sheep grazed the overgrown garden, the dilapidated fence their means of entry.

One corner of the building was still upright, the roof intact. A tarpaulin had been dragged over the doorway. They sidled around the corner, weighing up the pros and cons of entering.

"No one's come out yet. We've not been that quiet," said Flora.

"Sod the consequences. Let's go in."

They took a deep breath, walked up to the door and opened the curtain. Fergus took the first step through.

"All clear." Flora joined him.

The room held a blow-up mattress, sleeping bag, camping stove, mug, plate, knife and fork. Nothing else.

"Looks like someone's living here," said Flora.

"You don't say."

"Could be an old tramp."

"With a set up like this? Are you for real?"

"If you've a better idea let me know."

A wasp whizzed past Flora's ear, hovered and sped back.

It landed on her shirt. "Get that thing off me." She started to hyperventilate.

Fergus calmly walked up to her and batted the wasp away. "You're bigger than it."

"I don't sting." Then for good measure, "Or pester the bejeezes out of anyone."

"Wuss."

Flora kept watch. Fergus searched every nook and cranny. This didn't take long as both nooks and crannies were in short supply. Nothing screamed out at them saying, this room belongs to an international antiquities thief. It looked as though they'd wasted another day.

In one more desperate attempt, Fergus looked under the mattress and the sleeping bag. Nothing.

"Shake the sleeping bag out," said Flora.

Fergus did her bidding and a note fell out.

National Library of Scotland

"It's dated yesterday," said Fergus.

He stuffed the note back in the sleeping bag and rearranged it on the bed.

He glanced at his phone. No internet access.

"Come on. I need to get on the net."

They hot-footed it back to the quad bike and pointed it in the direction of Dundee.

Chapter 51

Back in Fergus's bedroom, they kicked off their shoes, grabbed cold drinks and fired up the computer. The internet proved what Fergus suspected. The news sites were flooded with it. A papyrus with a painting of the God Seth had been stolen from the National Library of Scotland the previous night.

"Who?" asked Flora. "Sounds a bit biblical for Ancient Egypt."

"He was the god of violence, storms and the desert."

"Your head must be exploding with all the trivia you've got stuffed in there."

"Photographic memory. I know more if you want it."

"Go on then. Wow me."

"Seth in the Bible was Adam's son. He succeeded his father when Cain killed Abel."

"I bow before you. I'm not worthy." Her actions echoed her words.

"Get up, you dozy mare."

She grinned and jumped up.

"I'll be conjuring up the wrath of Seth when this is over. He can do violence to Ahmed."

"Good plan. So, the farmhouse, the castle and the Mystery of the Cursed Dagger are all connected."

"Looks like."

"How are they getting in to all those museums? Your dad's got a key for Dundee. Not the rest of them."

"But he does."

"What!"

"He can get access to nearly every museum in Scotland. Some abroad as well. For his research."

"That's wicked."

"Not if they're saying you're nicking stuff, it's not."

"He's in the jail. How can he be on the rob?"

"Accomplices? He's giving them the keys? The police think so. Mum says they've charged him for withholding evidence."

"Your dad's deeper in the mire every minute."

"Don't remind me." His eyes shone with unshed tears.

"We'd better do something about it, then, Geekmeister."

Chapter 52

That was where the plan came unstuck. Inspiration had flown, leaving them alone and with no clue where to go next. Gloom descended and they sank into their own thoughts. In the absence of any better ideas they decided to go back to the castle. A stake-out seemed like a jolly good idea.

"Not tonight. The parents will be on our case big time if we're caught," said Fergus.

"If my mother notices," was Flora's contribution. Bella would miss her, though. She didn't want her sister to get worried.

Fergus was on a different quad bike the next morning. It was big, and black with a lightning streak. This did not paint a promising picture to a nervous Flora.

"Adair's out of town so he won't notice."

"And there's a reason for the transformation?"

"This one's faster. We'll be there in no time."

Flora shook her head nervously.

Fergus hastened to reassure her. "This is more stable than Murdoch's. You'll be fine."

Shoving aside thoughts of death and funerals, Flora climbed on.

Despite Fergus's reassurances, and his obvious delight in the journey, Flora spent the time holding on for dear life and promising herself, if she ever got there in one piece, she'd never ride a quad bike again! It was with a surge of relief that she struggled off the bike and back onto solid ground near the castle.

"It's still locked up tight," she observed.

"And deserted." Fergus surveyed the countryside.

"Should've brought something to do," said Flora.

"This is a stake-out, not a party," Fergus retorted. "Do you think Sherlock played games when he was on a case?"

"Actually he did. He played whist."

"You say there's a load of crap shoved in *my* brain. Use your phone for entertainment."

"No signal."

"I could tell you about the flora and fauna of the area."

"Forget it. I'll read a book." She picked up her phone.

They settled in among the trees. Nothing happened for some hours. Flora finished her book and started another one.

Their supplies were all gone and they were thinking of giving up when a van appeared. They hastily put phones away and peered through the bushes to watch the action.

The van doors opened and two men jumped out. There was a mini earthquake when the swarthy one landed with a thud. The other—Flora's ginger-haired man—was more nimble.

Flora leapt up to get a better look. A tug at her shirt had her back on her backside.

"You'll give us away. You're a nightmare on an investigation."

She contented herself with a quiet huff. The argument could wait till later.

Swarthy and Ginger had the front doors to the turret open. They nimbly carried a few small items inside. The next object required both of them. They trod carefully but still struggled. One end nearly dropped.

"Look out!"

Ginger steadied it again. They progressed at the speed of a striking slug.

"Is that a coffin?" Flora got ready to bolt.

"Probably. With a vampire in it."

"What? You're having a laugh."

"No. It's definitely a coffin."

The muscles in her face twitched.

Ginger pulled a phone out and spoke into it. Conversation finished, the ground shook as Swarthy stomped inside. He came out carrying a rucksack and climbed behind the wheel. Ginger locked up, checked the padlock and joined his mate. The van left.

"Hey! How did *he* manage to get a signal?" Flora asked indignantly, looking at her own phone. "*I* still can't get one!"

"Different carrier? Or perhaps they have satellite phones." Fergus shrugged.

The Detective Duo waited about half an hour before heading in the same direction as the van.

Driving down a narrow backroad at a cracking pace, Fergus swerved to avoid a tangle of cars in the lane. The bike headed straight for a copse of trees. They travelled a fair distance before Fergus managed to bring the bike to a standstill. Flora grabbed the handlebars as she bounced up from the seat. She smashed back into the saddle. Pain shrieked along her nerve endings threatening to explode in a molten ball of fire. She screamed in agony. Fergus fared better as he'd gripped hard with his knees.

"There's been an accident.," Fergus said, needlessly. "We should go help."

Flora was torn but edged towards helping. They climbed from the bike, took off their helmets and ran back to the scene, Flora somewhat tenderly rubbing her backside.

Two cars had been involved in the accident. The Audi A5 had a mangled bonnet, the mini a bent door. The acrid smell of steam, oil and crushed metal hung heavy on the air. Two men were slinging accusations at each other.

"That car was brand new. I'm suing you for every penny you've got." Red-faced and dapper, the driver stood with hands on hips.

"Brand new? I've seen more modern antiques." This one had a face like a boxer who had lost every fight since time began.

"You could have killed me."

"I wish I had, you stupid old sod. Blokes your age shouldn't be on the road."

Flora walked up to them. "Is there anything we can do to help? Would you like us to go to a garage?"

It was then the world changed.

Chapter 53

No sooner had Flora uttered the words than she was grabbed and a hand clamped over her mouth. The smell of what was sweat, or onions, or maybe pee mugged her nostrils. Her feet lashed out and connected with bone. A curse filled the air, and the hand clenched tighter. She fought for breath. No air in or out. A brief moment that felt like millennia, and the hand moved. Her lungs gulped the fresh Scottish air.

Fergus swung between helping and running. Possibilities flashed through his brain. Was fighting for Flora best? What if he ran and found help? First one way then the other. His foot moved to the same frantic drumbeat as his thoughts. No, he couldn't leave her. His airways tightened and a wheeze escaped. He pulled his inhaler from his pocket and inhaled a couple of puffs. Better to be ready for flight.

"Phones. Give 'em 'ere."

"You've a way with words, mister."

Fergus gave a warning shake of the head but too late. A resounding crack rang out as an enormous hand whacked Flora in the face. Boxer man meant business.

"Shut it, brat."

Flora's eyes widened in surprise, then filled with tears.

"Please, mister, let me text my sister. You can read it. She's disabled. She'll worry. Just to say I'm okay. Please. Please, mister." Her nose dripped blood. She wiped it away, smearing blood over her face and bare arm.

Boxer man nodded. He watched as she composed a text.

"I'm gonna be late Hell's Bells. No need to worry."

She no sooner pressed send than the enormous hand snatched the phone. Boxer man threw it on the ground and smashed it with a size sixteen hobnail boot.

"That's a top of the range phone. I've only had it five weeks."

"Stop snivelling. Who cares?"

Fergus's phone suffered a similar fate. In his case he'd only had it two days.

"Are you working for Ahmed?" said Flora.

"Who."

"Mr Minkey."

"Minkah." said Fergus.

The man shook his head. "Shut it."

Dapper and Boxer deftly tied their hands and feet. Another man, driving a Land Rover, arrived and they slung the prisoners in the back. Not a seatbelt in sight.

"If there's a crash, we'll be killed." said Fergus.

"Would the pair of you shut up? One more word, your mouths get taped."

A bone-jarring trip and a multitude of bruises later, they arrived at their prison.

Chapter 54

Well, I guess we got our wish."

"To be tied up and a prisoner?"

"Do be brief, Fergus."

They were sitting on a cold stone floor. The place was dry but smelt like old clothes and rotten wood.

They peered around in the gloom. The lone window was small, high up and filthy.

"There's a lot of stuff in here."

"Eloquently put." Fergus stretched his long legs out in front of him.

"Oh, sorry for not being more specific. Seein' as we can't make anything out, it's difficult for me to name the 'stuff.'"

"Touchy." More of a squeak than a word.

Another wriggle of her bum got Flora into a more comfortable position. For how long? There were only a few ways to sit when bound hand and foot. An attempt to stand up was fruitless and resulted in her head bouncing off the wall.

"Ow!"

"Watch out. If you end up in a coma, we'll never get out of here."

"In a coma! What?"

"Apart from injuring yourself, got any bright ideas?"

"They'll be looking for us."

"Er, no one knows we're missing, genius."

"I've sent the code."

"What code, Mata Hari?"

"To Bella. The text message."

"How did you slip a code under Boxer and Dapper? What did that text say?"

"'I'm gonna be late Hell's Bells'. I taught Bella never to use Hell's Bells in a text unless it was an emergency. She'll tell an adult."

"Flora, you really are a freaking genius." He considered it further. "Have you got location services on?"

"Yup. They'll know where we were kidnapped."

Fergus allowed himself a few whoops and hollers.

Then a silence as thick as Dundee fog descended.

Flora shifted. A cloud of dust rose up, resulting in several sneezes and a fresh nose bleed. Bright red blood dripped onto her shorts. She sniffed. The blood slid down her throat, leaving a coppery taste.

"I feel sick," she moaned.

Fergus looked at her as well as he could in the gloom.

"Don't lie down or you'll choke on your vomit," he advised helpfully.

"Idiot!"

After a few minutes, the bleeding stopped.

This was hell.

Chapter 55

We'll try and untie the ropes. Turn around," said Fergus. Flora was glad of the direction because she couldn't muster an original thought. Misery had that effect on her.

They shuffled and wriggled for several minutes until they were back to back.

"Put your Scout skills to the test, Geekmeister."

His Scout skills didn't help much when it came to untying knots blind, with his own hands tightly tied behind his back.

Despite the restricted movement, he picked away at the knot. Fibre by fibre it grew less tight. Painstaking. Slow. Pick. Pick. Pick.

The sound of the padlock bouncing off wood reverberated through their cavernous prison.

Frantic shuffling and they had their backs against the wall.

Dapper and Boxer stood in the doorway, silhouetted by the sun. They were carrying trays. Each held a sandwich and a plastic bottle of water. They deposited the trays on the floor and left.

"How do they expect us to eat that?" demanded Fergus in disgust.

"Dunno. Let's try and get the ropes off again."

They continued the assault on the ropes, but ten minutes later they were still tied up.

"I'm starving. We haven't got time for this," said Flora. "I don't want to starve to death in a turret in the middle of nowhere."

"You lift my sandwich as far as you can. I'll do the same for you."

Flora almost pulled her arms out of the sockets, but Fergus was able to wolf his sandwich down. He didn't even mind that it was ham. Flora nibbled at hers.

"You gotta eat, Flora."

"I still feel sick from the blood." She nibbled a bit more and then abandoned the food.

The water was a bit more tricky, but they managed to swallow a little. Too much of it simply poured down their clothes.

"Great. Now I'm wet *and* sticky with blood."

Fergus reapplied himself to knot loosening.

Flora wriggled.

"Stay still."

"I'm being bitten."

"Can't do much about midgies."

"This isn't midgies. OMG. They're swarming over the bloodstains."

Fergus felt something tickling his leg and looked down.

"Red ants. Formica Sanguinea, or slave maker ants, to be precise."

"I didn't think we got red ants in Bonnie Scotland."

"You do in Aberdeenshire."

"You for real? How do you know this?"

"If you want to be an archaeologist, you need to know about insects."

"You're fourteen years old." Her face flushed. "Get them off my clothes."

She moved like a caterpillar dancing the tango.

"It's okay. I'll sort it."

Fergus did his best to get the worst of them off. It only provided temporary respite. Returning to the knot loosening, he had to stop periodically to sweep ants. As time moved on, much to Flora's relief, the ants were more interested in the remains of the sandwich than blood. They bore away their spoils of war and left her in peace.

Darkness fell long before the first knot gave up the struggle. Aching and exhausted, they stopped. The rest of the knots would wait until the first faltering glimmer of light appeared. Silence fell. A fitful sleep bore them to places other than kidnap castle.

Chapter 56

The next morning, Flora's stomach growled noisily and she regretted her squeamishness. She could murder that sandwich now. Not a crumb remained after the invasion of the ants. At least they still had some water to slake their thirst.

"You stink of blood," Fergus said, wrinkling his nose.

"Oh, and you're a supermodel? Get off your high horse. You don't exactly smell sweet yourself."

"Touché."

"D'you even know what that means?"

"Course—"

"Get these knots untied before Bubble and Squeak come back."

A couple of hours later, Fergus's fingers were bleeding but he'd done his job.

Flora tugged her hands out of the loose bindings.

"Well done, titch. Now you untie me."

She flexed her fingers. "Flaming Nora. You might have to wait for a wee while."

Fergus sighed and rested his back on the wall.

She attempted to unknot her ankle ropes. Her fingers refused to cooperate. She waited; tried again. Finally, she got them off her ankles.

"You're going to have to wait, bestie. My hands are killing me."

"See what's around. There might be something to cut the ropes with."

Rubbing her hands, she stumbled over to the first box.

Tugging the lid had no effect. She stuck her nails under and pulled. That resulted in pain and a broken nail. The lid stayed put. Another box was covered in a grubby sheet. She yanked it off and screamed.

"I *told* you that was a coffin."

"It's not a coffin—it's a *sarcophagus!*" Fergus shouted.

"Same freaking difference. We're still entombed with a dead body."

She dropped the cloth and ran over to Fergus and worked frantically at his ropes.

Precisely seventeen minutes later he was no longer bound.

Chapter 57

The boxes they could open showed countless treasures; cows and gods, nestled next to jewellery, urns and papyrus. Not just Egypt was represented, but Scotland and Rome also, according to the Geekmeister.

The only place they didn't look was inside the sarcophagus. Even Fergus balked at that. Flora flat out refused. She explained painstakingly that she would put his dead body in it if he opened it up. That was enough to sway him towards the right decision.

"This bunch of lunatics are gonna kill us. There's no way they're letting us away with serious cash like this involved. They're gonna kill us. I'll never see Bella or Charlie again."

"Flora MacDonald, call on the Jacobite within. Your ancestor's blood runs through your veins."

"Most of my blood's on my shirt." She straightened up and pushed her hair back. "Let's do this. We're going to escape. Go for it, Geekmeister."

The escape had to wait while they answered a call of nature. Flora had waited for a bladder busting length of time before she gave in. A dark spot hidden by boxes was employed as a temporary toilet. Fergus could hear the gushing and splashing of urine as she pee'd on the floor. Even famous detectives had to do the most mundane of tasks. He whistled 'Scotland the Brave' to drown out the sound.

Chapter 58

The Detective Duo got back to detecting. Or escaping. They were way past the stage of detecting. They heaved, shoved and dragged a solid wood table over to the window. Fergus stood on it but still couldn't see out. Flora clambered up beside him. He hoisted her up until she could peer out. She just about made it.

"Anything there?" he asked.

"Difficult to tell through the dirt. Don't think there're any cars. Can't get a good view of the door though." She leaned in closer and tried to look around.

"Do you think there's a heavy guarding the door?"

"Could be. *I* would leave one."

Fergus hoisted her higher. Teetered. Moved one foot, to stabilise himself. The table wobbled and he lost his balance. Flora thumped on to the table. He landed on the floor. There was a sound of something breaking. He stood up, rubbing his bum. He reached into his pocket and pulled out several pieces of hard blue plastic. Then a dented metal tube.

"That your inhaler?"

"Sure was. You okay?"

"Super. No thanks to you."

"You're heavier than you look." Fergus tried his legs out with a few steps. The only damage seemed to be to his backside. *I'll have a bruise the size of Scotland by tomorrow.*

"Are you saying I'm fat?"

"No. Stop changing the subject. You're driving me nuts."

"I know one thing." She paused.

"Spit it out. We'll die of old age if I don't kill you first."

"We aren't getting out of this window. It's sealed."

"Considering we can't reach it, it's a moot point."

"We could've built a—"

"You're wasting time. Think about what we can do."

"Can we get out the hatch at the back?"

They crossed over to it and took a closer look.

"Can't see a thing," said Fergus.

"If this was the Famous Five, they'd have matches in their rucksacks. They'd use wood from the boxes to produce a fiery torch."

"Thanks for that. I'll carry matches around with me in future."

"Don't Scouts know how to produce fire from a couple of bits of wood?"

"Not any more. 'Sides, I'd probably burn the place down."

Fergus felt all around the hatch. They heard a car and rushed back to the ropes. The ankle ropes were wrapped round and tucked in to make them tight. They shoved their hands behind their backs.

The door opened to reveal a completely different pair of thugs. One of them was shorter than Flora and covered in tattoos. There didn't seem to be an inch of skin that hadn't been inked. They threw a couple of plastic wrapped sandwiches at them. The sandwiches were joined by four large bottles of water. Tattoo guy and his mate lifted a box each and carried them through the door. The sound of slamming wood and a rattling padlock accompanied their return to semi-darkness.

"Sherlock would've fought them," said Flora.

"Sherlock wasn't fourteen years old. He was also a bare knuckle fighter."

Flora shook her head.

They fell upon the food and washed it down with water. Flora was a tad hesitant when it came to the water, but in the end she decided they'd be back in Dundee before she needed the loo again.

The hatch awaited. Fergus felt around again. He thumped it hard but it wasn't shifting.

"Let's find something heavy. We'll smash it."

"That went so well last time."

"Why are you so critical?"

Flora stomped off. "Are you coming to help me find something to smash the door down then? Seein' as you're so keen on the idea and all?"

Chapter 59

A quick conflab, a couple of high fives, and an escape committee of two was formed. Tearing boxes open led to broken nails and bloody fingers, but it was worth it. They lifted out antiquities and examined each piece for its usefulness in supporting the escape plan. Nothing suitable jumped out at them, and one by one the pieces were laid to one side. Flora looked up as though she thought a guardian angel would appear from the sky. That didn't help either. All that appeared from the sky was a spider. They searched box after box. It was hot and dirty work.

"We need to get better at research. There's loads here we didn't account for," said Flora. "We're not that good at detecting." She wiped sweat from her brow.

"From this lot, I'd say they've been at this for a while."

Throughout the exchange the search continued.

In the end Fergus said, "Nothing for it. We'll have to use one of the bigger statues."

"Not happenin'. They could be worth squillions of dosh."

"It's either that or be stuck in here forever. Or more likely dead."

"Which statue?"

It had to be big and heavy, but not so heavy that they couldn't lift it between them. Only one statue fitted the bill: an ugly representation of a goddess.

"Well, Hathor, I hope you'll forgive us for pressing you into service," said Fergus.

Fergus used all his strength to heave the statue at the

hatch. The door buckled, but held firm. The same could not be said for the statue. The horns broke off immediately. The head teetered for a moment and followed the horns. A crack appeared in the torso.

Fergus and Flora stood looking at it with wide eyes.

"We'll have no pocket money for the rest of our lives," said Fergus. "We are so dead."

"The goddess died for a noble cause," said Flora. She rearranged her face in a suitably sombre look.

"RIP, Hathor. You served us well." Fergus put his hand on his heart. Then he stooped back to the hatch and ran his hand over it again. "Ouch."

He stood up and sucked his finger, then bent right down and examined the hatch closely.

"I think our bashing has loosened the screws in the hinges."

He tried opening it with a sharp piece of the broken statue. "I can't even get it in the thingy bit where you turn the screwdriver."

"The Geekmeister doesn't know everything, then."

Fergus thought for a minute and dashed back to where they had been sitting. He picked something up.

"What's that?"

He ignored her and bent to his task. The sliver of blue plastic was doing the trick. Progress was slow but eventually the screws were out of the hinges, and they were able to push the trapdoor out.

"Move, now." Fergus hoisted her out through the trapdoor and followed suit.

"Run."

Adrenalin made Flora's legs pump faster. They covered the open ground and disappeared into the trees. They kept up the frantic pace. Fergus indicated the direction to the main road.

Neither of them stopped until they flagged down a car.

Sanctuary.

Chapter 60

O r not, as they soon found out. Boxer was driving the car. Tattoo guy was in the passenger seat. Rope magically appeared and was applied liberally. Back in the back seat they went.

Flora was squirming all the way back.

"I need the loo."

Boxer dragged her to a ruined part of the castle. "There you go." He untied the ropes.

"I'm not going with you watching me."

"Don't push your luck. Either go or back in the castle."

He half turned and she performed. Ropes back on, she was dragged into the turret. A bucket was brought in from the car. This time their hands were tied in front. Boxer went out to the car and returned with some bottles of water for the prisoners and the means to attach a temporary cover to the hatch.

"Try to escape again and I'll shackle you to the wall."

He strode off and they were left in their prison.

"On the bright side," said Flora. "If they're feeding us doesn't look like they're planning to bump us off."

"I hope you're right."

They were back to the long wait.

"I feel grotty," said Flora.

"Ill?"

"Filthy dirty. I smell worse than the Fithie Burn when the water's low."

"The smell of mouldy blood is rank."

"Shall we play 'I Spy'?"

"We're not two."

"Okay, brainbox. Entertain me with tales of archaeological digs."

They'd worked their way through Egypt and were in Israel when the door opened.

.

Chapter 61

A man walked through the door, flanked by Dapper and Boxer. He was bald. Completely bald. Fergus started.

"Uncle Gerunt. Have you been taken prisoner too?"

Gerunt, wearing cargo shorts and a designer polo shirt, wasn't acting like a prisoner. He was acting like he owned the place.

"What are you doing here? Have you come to save us?" Fergus added. He attempted to stand up.

"Not at all. Quite the opposite, in fact."

Flora really did try to keep her mouth shut but the words came out anyway. "You're part of this."

"Give the girl a cuddly toy."

"But why? What would you do this for?" said Fergus.

"I'm the one to ask why. Why are you pair meddling in my affairs?"

"To be fair, we didn't know you were involved," said Flora. "Of course we'd definitely have kept out of it if we'd known you were on the rob."

"Don't be so impertinent, young lady."

Boxer smacked Flora in the face again.

She burst into tears as the bleeding started up again. "You're nothing but a great big bully. Leave me alone."

Boxer moved towards her. Gerunt put his arm out to stop him. He pulled a dazzling white linen handkerchief from his pocket. "Here, clean yourself up."

Flora took it and pressed it to her nose. The bleeding soon stopped. One eye was already black, she knew. She had a sinking feeling the other would soon be keeping it company.

Tears streamed down Fergus's face. He strained at his bonds and tried to stand up. "Why would you do this to my dad? You're best mates. What's our family ever done to you?"

"Everything comes so easily to your father. He always gets what he wants."

"What? I don't understand."

"He always gets the best digs, the fame, the acclaim. I get no recognition for my work."

"You're an antique dealer. It's not world saving." Flora's swollen nose was giving her gyp in the pain and voice department.

This time Gerunt let Boxer have his way. He hauled her up and slammed her against the wall. "One more word out of your mouth and you'll lose teeth."

Flora's parents had spent a fortune on her bonnie white teeth. She made a decision to keep her mouth shut.

He let her go and she slid down the wall, landing with a thump. Her backside joined the pain dance that was going on all over her body.

"I get very little in the way of remuneration, either," Gerunt continued as though there had been no interruption.

"We're not that rich ourselves."

"Your father's a millionaire."

Flora's eyes widened and she looked at Fergus. "We didn't find any evidence of that!"

"First I've heard of it as well." He turned to Gerunt. "What are you going to do with us?"

"I haven't yet decided. You'll be the first to know when I do." He swivelled towards the boxes and considered the mess with narrowed eyes.

Dapper lugged a toolbox over to the hatch. "Boss. You'll want to see this."

Gerunt took one look at the broken statue and exploded.

"You despicable pair of worms. What have you done?"

"It was an accident."

Gerunt moved over and booted Fergus. "That statue was worth over a million pounds. What have you got to say for yourself?"

"It wasn't your statue, anyway. You don't have to worry about the price," said Fergus.

Another boot and Fergus started to shake.

"Stop kicking him. His inhaler's broken."

"Do you think I care? Nefertiti's dying and you broke one of the most expensive pieces we have."

"Nef's dying? What? How?"

"She needs treatment in America. It comes at a price. Your little efforts just might have killed her."

With that he walked out of the door and left them in the dark once more.

Chapter 62

"Who's Nefertiti? Apart from an Egyptian Queen, that is?"

"I can't believe she's dying. She's younger than me. What have we *done*, Flora?"

"We haven't done anything. Who is she?"

"One of Uncle Gerunt's daughters. *No*—I'm *not* going to call him Uncle any more. How *dare* he." He started coughing.

"Steady, tiger. What's this about your dad being a millionaire?"

"I don't think he is. Don't know why he said that."

"Wouldn't it be so cool if he was?"

"Don't get your hopes up. Even if he is, I don't think he's gonna splash the cash. He hasn't done it up till now. Besides, we saw the stuff on his computer that says otherwise."

They still had to get out of their prison. No, make that out of the ropes. The knot picking restarted. Thread by painful thread, Fergus pulled on the knots. They stopped for a drink. Flora tried washing her face with the hanky and some water. That merely produced a rather streaked brown effect on both her face and the cloth.

Fergus rinsed his hands, and returned to the knots.

"This is going nowhere. Is there a sharp stone anywhere?"

"Lots on the walls."

"Find one and rub the knots on it."

They did this for hours before collapsing, exhausted.

"It wasn't like this in the *Hardy Boys* or *Nancy Drew*," said Flora.

"That lot got out of everything just by blinking. Obviously had superpowers."

"I'm beginning to think those books are a load of crap. Nancy Drew didn't have a hair out of place."

"Your hair's covered in blood."

Flora wasn't listening. She'd fallen asleep. Within ten minutes she was snoring fit to burst eardrums. Blocked noses had that effect.

Fergus curled up and joined her in the land of dreams. Or was that nightmares? Their twitching bodies seemed to indicate it was.

Chapter 63

Vigorous rubbing on sharp stones resulted in scrapes and bruises—and eventual freedom. They rubbed their hands and feet to ease excruciating pins and needles. When they could stand, they stamped their feet hard.

If they wanted to escape, they needed something to unscrew the hinges. They'd searched the place from top to bottom already. There was nothing for it but the sarcophagus. Flora swallowed hard and hobbled over.

Flora took a deep breath and they lifted the lid. They were surprised at how light it was and how easy to lift. There was a mummy inside. Flora breathed in hard through her mouth. No joy. She breathed harder. The world went black and she collapsed on the floor.

She came to, spluttering.

"What are you doing, you stupid sod. Stop it! You'll kill me." She stood up and took the water bottle from Fergus, taking a swig before setting it on the ground. "Let's do this."

They both grabbed the side of the sarcophagus and leaned over. The mummy looked well preserved. A small bag lay on its chest.

"Could be its entrails."

Flora swallowed hard to stop the vomit that was rising up in her throat. "Open it."

"You sure?"

A slight nod. Then stronger.

Fergus reached in his hand and lifted out the package. He

unwrapped it layer by layer. When he reached the end, they were staring at the dagger.

Neither spoke. The silenced lengthened. Several long seconds which stretched into infinity.

Then. "OMG. We're gonna die. We've touched the dagger. Put it down. Throw it away. We're cursed."

Fergus, face white, said, "For goodness' sake, calm down. If we're being honest, *I've* touched it. *I* might be cursed."

"You can't be cursed. Put it back. Put the lid on."

"The curse hasn't got us until now."

They both stared at the dagger again.

"It's got a nice blade for unscrewing the hinges."

"The dagger? You're going to use the cursed dagger? The most expensive antiquity in the world?"

In the absence of anything better, this was exactly what he planned to do.

It was time to defy the curse.

The damaged hatch did not quite fit any more. There was a glimmer of light. The gold lit up and shone as it twisted in Fergus's hand. Gentle at first, he used increasing pressure. Dapper may have been slight but his handiwork showed his real strength. One particular screw would not budge. He grasped the handle tighter and put all his power into it. With the ringing sound of tortured metal, the blade of the dagger snapped. A scream filled the air. Then silence.

Flora and Fergus stared at each other in horror. What had they unleashed?

"Did you hear—?" Fergus hesitated.

"I think," said Flora slowly, "that might have been the curse escaping. D'you think we might have released it from its job?"

"You have some imagination, Flora MacDonald."

Chapter 64

The handle was thrown to one side and Fergus continued using the blade. His hands started to shake. Flora took over and soon the hatch was free. The blade joined the handle. They climbed out through the hatch.

Their feet were in motion the minute they touched the ground. They had to outrun the curse.

Flora thought of Bella. Had the police been called? Was Bella worried? Or scared? She wanted to see Bella more than anything else. And her mum. She wanted her mum.

The thought of his dad being released from prison kept Fergus's feet moving. He wanted his family together again. How could Uncle Gerunt do this? It was difficult to think of him as anyone other than his uncle. A man who had read him bedtime stories as a child. Answered all his questions about antiques. Looked after him when he got hurt. His dad was going to be devastated. Stress and exercise tightened Fergus's airways. The wheeze increased. His pace decreased.

"Flora." He mustered up all the breath he had. A coughing fit tore at him and he stopped.

Flora realised Fergus wasn't with her. She turned back.

"Let's get you hidden. I'll go for help."

The immediate area was devoid of hiding places.

"Wait here." She darted off.

Ten minutes later she was back. "Come on." She half dragged him to the perfect spot. She shoved him inside a hollow tree.

"I'll get the police." She looked at Fergus. "And an ambulance."

She ran without looking back. Better not think about what could happen to Fergus. Not with that curse out there. Better to think about helping.

Chapter 65

With a nose stuffed full of dried blood, Flora struggled to breathe as she ran as fast as she could. Soon the blood started dripping again. She stopped and held her nose tight until the bleeding ceased then forced herself to put one foot in front of the other. After about fifteen minutes, she realised she didn't know where she was. Or where the quad bike was. She clenched her sweaty palms, breathed deeply and looked around.

Climbing a small hummock, she studied her surroundings. She could see for some distance. Nothing looked familiar. She forced herself to focus on what was in the near distance. Far distance just made her dizzy. Trees. Were any of them different? What did she know? Not a lot when it came to trees. She bit her lip in frustration.

She could see the main road clearly. Maybe she should go down there and ask for help. But look how that had turned out last time! She dismissed the idea and turned her gaze back to the terrain. She cast her mind back to the crash site. How had they driven back? In her mind she could picture being driven up a slope. Was that a clear or a false memory? Definitely real. Her back was pressed into the back of the seat. So definitely up.

In reverse the slope was downwards. She searched the landscape and spotted a slope. Fear gave her the feet of a goat, the braveness of a lion and the speed of a cheetah as she dashed towards it.

Whether by luck or by good judgment she would never

know, but somehow she found her way back to the forest where they had left the quad bike. She could see it peeping from the foliage where they'd left it. She dashed in its direction and tripped. There was that nose bleed again. She didn't have time to worry about it. Let it bleed. She wiped it with the hem of her T-shirt. It was ruined anyway.

Then she realised someone was coming after her. Not someone, but two people. She knew that hummock had been a mistake. Not only could she see: she could also be seen.

Chapter 66

Reaching the quad bike, Flora grabbed a helmet from the pannier and crammed it on her head. She clambered on. Her hand shook as she reached for the key. It took her a couple of attempts to grip it and turn. The all-terrain vehicle roared into life. She could feel the power and the deep thrumming of the engine under her body. Her legs felt weak with the vibration. She clamped her feet tightly on the step and settled her body more firmly into the saddle. Then she remembered she needed one foot to push the gear lever. She wasn't going anywhere without that. Kicking with her right foot resulted in the bike moving forward. Then it stalled. She repeated this three times. "Come on. Come *on*." Noticing her white knuckles, she loosened her death grip on the handles. "Relax, Flora. And breathe."

She heard crashing coming ever nearer as her captors sprinted through the trees. She made one more attempt. The bike moved off and held its course. She heard a faint pop and something whizzed past her head. *They're shooting at me*. She kicked a couple of times and the quad bike picked up speed.

She rattled and bumped over rutted tracks, moor, undergrowth and a few rocks. She swerved around a huge one and nearly fell off. The quad bike teetered on the verge of overturning but righted itself with a bone-shattering thud. Knowing that she had to save Fergus was the only thing that kept her going. She could almost hear the thumping of her heartbeat over the roar of the bike. This was not her idea of a good time. She swore to herself she was never investigating another thing. Ever.

She outstripped her pursuers and began to relax a little and the going became a little easier as her body worked with, rather than against, the bike. She came to the outskirts of Dundee. This was a built-up area, and she was more likely to get caught by the rozzers. What should she do? Given this was an emergency, she decided to belt caution completely out of the court and use the dual carriageway. This was terrifying. The smell of car fumes made her sick. Lorries thundered past at alarming speed, threatening to overturn her. After what seemed like hours she arrived at Bell Street Police Station. Only then did she realise she'd driven past several police stations to get there.

She pushed through the door and shouted. "I need the police and an ambulance." Then promptly vomited all over the floor.

Chapter 67

She found herself surrounded by several police officers, and a cleaner. The cleaner wielded a mop and the officers took her through to the back. They asked her a zillion questions.

All the time she kept repeating, "You've got to find Fergus."

No matter what way they asked her, she couldn't tell them exactly where Fergus was. The pair had been reported missing. 'Find my iPhone' had sent a message to Apple saying where the phone had been. There had been police crawling all over the place.

"I'll have to take you."

They took swabs from her face, her nose and the scratches on her face.

A kind female officer, wielding a first-aid box, came in. She wiped Flora's face and cuts. Dressings were placed on the worst ones.

All the while, Flora shouted, "We've got to find Fergus."

She explained about his asthma. She explained about the curse. She explained she was terrified he'd die. They still insisted she was sorted out first.

Clean clothes were found from somewhere and she changed. Hers were taken into evidence.

There was a squad car waiting outside. Her dad clattered through the door just as she was being escorted to the car.

"Flora. Thank God you're all right." He hugged her so tight she thought her ribs would break. "Where are you taking her?"

The police asked him to step aside. They would like a word with him.

When they came back, he said. "Find Fergus. Look after yourself. I'll be at the hospital when you get there."

"Let Rad know what's happening?" Flora said to her father. The police said he should leave that to them.

"I'll make sure Rad's looked after. Don't you worry, Flora."

If she hadn't felt so wretched, the journey would have been exciting. It wasn't often a teen got a ride in a police car. Not unless they were on the wrong side of the law. Maybe they'd take her to task for her illegal use of a quad bike later. She swallowed hard and pushed the thought away. As the blue lights flashed and the sirens blared, she managed to direct them to vaguely the right spot. The ruined castle part helped.

When they arrived, police swarmed from the squad cars. Flora climbed out and if it hadn't been for a delightful female police officer, she would have collapsed. Flora didn't know she could ever be in so much pain. This detecting lark was not what it was made out to be. The ambulance arrived and two paramedics leapt out at the back. A stretcher followed. Fergus was still where she'd left him.

Flora insisted that she went in the ambulance with him. It was obvious she needed treatment as well so the paramedics agreed. Her tame policewoman came as well. That was non-negotiable.

She very soon changed her mind about being in the ambulance but it was too late. They were hooking Fergus up to all sorts of machines and tubes. He had an oxygen mask on. The oxygen made a high pitched hissing noise as it went through some liquid.

"Hang in there, Geekmeister. The police and ambulance have come riding to the rescue. You're gonna be okay."

She turned to the policewoman. "He *is* gonna be okay, isn't he?"

"Of course he is. He looks like a fighter to me."

Chapter 68

When they arrived, Fergus was wheeled into one cubicle and Flora into another. They were reunited an hour later. By that time Fergus had perked right up. Rad, still wearing her painting clothes, was in the cubicle with him. She leapt up and gave Flora a hug.

"Thanks for looking after my boy."

"He looked after me. We'd never have gotten out without him."

"Flora, I wouldn't go after any modelling gigs for a while. You're not looking your best."

Whatever they were doing to treat Fergus it had worked.

"At least I don't smell anymore. Can't say the same for you."

"I nearly died. I'll take being smelly if it means I'm not dead."

"The police said something about Gerunt being involved in this," said Rad.

The Detective Duo gave her the full story with many interruptions, backtracking and flourishes.

Rad shook her head. "I don't believe it. He's been our friend since university. We trusted him."

The police came in to say that they'd captured everyone. "Your descriptions of Dapper, Boxer, Tattoo Guy and his mate were spot on."

"Is Dad getting out of prison? I really want to see him."

"Not yet, son. We'll need to convince the Sheriff before that can happen."

Chapter 69

Flora was dragged back to her cubicle. The nurses hadn't finished cleaning her up before she'd sneaked out of her cubicle to find Fergus. In fact, not a lot had happened at all. *S'pose I'm not high priority with all the emergencies they get round here.* Soft gauze was used to wash the wounds and then comfortable dressings applied. She was wheeled off for x-rays. Photographs were taken of every inch of her body. She was poked and prodded by doctors and had every orifice examined.

Bella came hurtling through the curtains and stopped dead when she saw Flora. She shuffled from one foot to the other.

"Cat got your tongue, Hell's Bells?"

"Did I do good, Flora?"

Flora hugged her till she squirmed. "You did more than good. You are the bestest sister ever."

Bella's beam could have lit the Caird Hall and half the Christmas lights. "I did what you told me. I knew the code and I went to Mummy."

"You're a trooper, Bella."

"I'm glad you're okay, Flora. I was worried. So was Mummy."

Flora found this hard to believe and yet her mother was walking towards her. Flora could swear those were tears.

"Flora MacDonald, you were told not to get into this." The words were sharp, her actions soft. She pulled Flora into a hug and kissed the top of her head. "Don't you ever do that to me again. You mean too much to me."

The words flabber and gasted sprang to Flora's mind. Still she clung on to her mother. It was good to feel safe.

The next thought that entered Flora's befuddled brain was that her mother was sober. Maybe she should get kidnapped more often.

"I didn't know about that code, Flora. Truly brilliant idea. Well done."

"Thanks."

Her mother was still holding her hand. "What have the doctors said?"

"Nothing yet."

A nurse appeared through the curtain. She was holding a sheet of paper that she gave to Flora's mum. "She's free to go. Bring her back tomorrow to have the dressings changed."

Her mum helped her from the couch. It was a struggle to walk. She seemed to have seized up since she'd seen Fergus.

"Wait here."

She was left with Bella. She could hear raised voices. One of them sounded suspiciously like her mum.

A wheelchair appeared through the door, closely followed by her mother. "Hop in."

"Mum, can I borrow your phone? Mine got crushed. By a hobnail boot."

She was handed the phone with no lecture. Blimey, her mum must be worried.

She logged in to her app and discovered there were about a trillion squillion messages. The whole world was talking about them. It would appear all the injured and ill were recovering and people were starting to say the curse wasn't real.

Maybe, just maybe, breaking that blade had also broken the curse.

Chapter 70

Fergus had been taken to the ward. Flora's mother agreed to take her to see him.

"Am I glad to see you," he said. "This lot won't stop fussing."

"This lot's your mother," said Rad tartly. "Don't be cheeky, Fergus." Despite the sharp words, she gently stroked his hair back from his head.

Fergus shook her hand off. "Sorry, Mum." He was grinning.

"What I'm still confused about," said Flora, "is how Ahmed fits into all of this."

"Yeah. Has he been arrested, Mum?"

"You pair are obsessed with Ahmed. Would you give the poor man a break!"

"Give him a break! I'd like to break both his kneecaps."

"That is quite enough, young man. I know you're ill but that is no excuse for rudeness."

"I think he was being quite polite, considering," said Flora. "Have you forgotten your husband's in prison?"

"Not any more, I'm not. The Sheriff released me." A smiling Duncan walked through the door, with Ahmed just a couple of paces behind him.

"What's *he* doing here?" demanded Fergus.

"You pair have some apologising and a lot of grovelling to do."

Fergus and Flora looked at each other with raised eyebrows.

"Ahmed will explain."

Ahmed bowed. "You have been causing me a great deal of trouble, Master Fergus, and Miss Flora."

He pressed his hands together and raised them to his mouth. A tilt of the head. He thought for a moment. "And yet you were right."

"We knew it."

"We *knew* we were right."

The Detective Duo high fived. Then it dawned on them.

"So why are you here and not in the nick?" asked Flora.

"Because I am the Egyptian Antiquity Police. I was running the investigation."

He laughed at the expressions on their faces.

"You made my work more difficult, my young friends. Not only was I chasing a gang, but I had to keep both of you out of trouble."

A quizzical look appeared on Flora's face. "Was it you watching me on the *Unicorn* that day?"

"It was indeed, young lady."

"My, you're good at your job."

"Thank you."

"So how come Dad got arrested? You must have known it wasn't him."

"It really looked as if my old friend was guilty. I was worried that this would be the case. This would have been disappointing."

"I like your turn of phrase, Ahmed," said Duncan. "I'd have said it would have been an unmitigated disaster."

"Where does Uncle Gerunt come into all of this? I still don't understand that."

"I can't get my head around it either," said Flora.

Duncan was silent for a few minutes as though considering whether to tell them or not. In the end he said, "Gerunt lived a lifestyle he couldn't afford. He was in debt up to his eyeballs and then Nef was diagnosed with a rare illness. He needed to raise millions of pounds to have her treated in America."

He stopped. Fergus and Flora were staring at him transfixed. Fergus shuffled slightly in his bed.

Ahmed took up the tale. "The local police were already on the case of thefts of antiquities. When the exhibition came to Scotland, they asked for our involvement. My relationship with your father meant I was the obvious choice. It would seem Gerunt stepped up his efforts when our rare antiquities came to your beautiful country."

"I think you pair owe Ahmed an apology," said Rad.

"I'm really sorry, Mr. Minkah," said Flora. She put her hand out and the Arab shook it gravely.

"Me too, Ahmed," said Fergus. "I'm afraid we broke a couple of the artefacts. The dagger was one of them."

"The other one was an ugly statue."

"If you are talking about the Goddess Hathor, young lady, then I agree. She was rather ugly. Do not worry, my young friends. The dagger will be fixed, as will Hathor."

Fergus and Flora couldn't believe it. They'd been detecting the detective. There was no more to be said.

The Fergus and Flora Mysteries

The Haunted Broch

While Fergus and Flora are assisting at an archaeological dig uncovering a long lost Scottish Broch, a series of unnatural sightings and unusual events have many of the dig team fleeing for their lives.

Fergus and Flora are catapulted into a mystery pitting their wits against supernatural beings to save the Broch and their friends on the team.

Book 2 in the Fergus and Flora Mysteries coming in 2017